Riding Through Life

Riding through Life

Aftermath and Kensi's Wedding

By J. Lynn Lombard

Cover design by Crimson Syn

Editing by Sarah DeLong and DeLong Words Editing and Proofreading

Riding Through Life   J. Lynn Lombard

Secrets have the power to break someone

Aftermath

Asking Kensi to marry me is one of the best decisions I've made in my life. We're at a critical crossroads. I've been honest, but the weight of one secret threatens what we've built. Redemption is possible if I'm willing to face the consequences head-on, showing her that I'm committed to repairing the damage. It might take time, but if Kensi is my peace and chaos, she is worth fighting for. Can I redeem myself in time to say I do?

Kensi

Keeping a secret, especially with the wedding drawing near, can feel like a heavy weight on my shoulders. It's clear Aftermath and I have a deep connection, but honesty is essential to building a lasting bond. Will sharing this one last secret now help strengthen our relationship, or will it push things too far?

Hidden truths can tear Aftermath and Kensi apart before they even make it to the altar. Will Aftermath and Kensi allow these demons to destroy what they've built, or can they open fully and confront the truths they've been hiding and ride through the storm and come out stronger on the other side?

Riding Through Life   J. Lynn Lombard

Chapter 1

Aftermath

Kensi looks exquisite in the leather skirt, black high-heeled boots and a sheer white top over a black bra that shows her flat stomach, which she's wearing just for me. My heart skips a beat when Kensi's multi-colored eyes are pinned on me as she sways her hips to the seductive music pumping through the speakers in our bedroom.

Sitting on our king-size bed, I swallow hard when Kensi saunters across the floor and kneels between my spread legs. She leans forward, giving me a glimpse of her ample cleavage making my mouth water. This woman has challenged me from the beginning of our story, and I wouldn't want it any other way. Kensi is the Yin to my Yang. My mother adores her, my club members cherish her and the other Ol' Ladies love her.

I stop Kensi's strip tease before I lose my will, and she takes over my ways. "Kensi, hold on for a second." Grabbing her arms to halt her forward progress

Riding Through Life   J. Lynn Lombard

of grinding on my aching shaft, I kiss her slowly to stop the sting of my words.

"What's wrong?" Kensi is breathing hard, her chest rising and falling in rapid motion.

"Nothing's wrong. I need you to stay still for a moment." I growl when she starts moving her ass against me.

"I don't want still, Mark. I need you." Kensi responds breathlessly.

And by all that is holy and from the love of God, I restrain myself from having my wicked ways with her delectable body. I set her on the bed next to me.

"What's going on?" Kensi asks, staring right at me making my heart beat hard against my chest.

I refrain from wiping the sweat forming on my brow and swallow hard. Gathering courage, I drop to one knee. "Kensi Donovan, I have been trying to find the right time to do this, but every time I get up the courage, something happens." I pull the black ring box out of my pocket and open it. I stare at the simple but exquisitely beautiful ring before looking at her. "I've searched far and long for a woman who completes me. One who challenges me in every way and keeps me on my toes. One who understands the biker's way of life and is willing to embrace it daily. You, Kensi Donovan, are the woman I've been searching for." I turn the box around and look into her eyes, one blue and one green, swelling with tears. "Will you make me the happiest biker in the world and marry me?"

Riding Through Life   J. Lynn Lombard

"Are you shitting me right now?" Kensi asks. A big smile lights up her face. I shake my head. "Is this for real?"

"One hundred percent real. So, will you?" Holding my breath waiting for her to answer, I steady my shaking hands.

"Yes, yes, a thousand times, yes." Kensi tackles me to the ground before I can put the ring on her finger. "I love you, Mark."

"I love you, Kensi."

Forgetting about the strip tease Kensi was giving me moments ago, I peel her clothes off and make love to my fiancée for the rest of the night.

Riding Through Life   J. Lynn Lombard

Chapter 2

Kensi

"I'm getting married!" I shout when I see Nadia with Matthew on her hip the next day in the kitchen at the Clubhouse. When she turns in my direction, I wiggle my left ring finger. I've never been subtle about anything and that isn't going to start now. I'm loud, brash and full of life and won't let anyone change that about me.

Last night after Aftermath proposed to me, he wouldn't let me use my phone and call someone or leave the room. He made love to me all night long. In the shower, on the floor, in the bed, and even in the closet when I was trying to get dressed this morning. That man has made me come so many times through the night, I'm surprised I can walk today.

I don't tell Nadia this though as she grabs my hand and a smile graces her lips. "Congratulations! When are you thinking?" Nadia asks.

"New Year's Eve." I'm so excited I doubt I'll be able to concentrate on anything today and that won't be productive for anyone.

Riding Through Life   J. Lynn Lombard

"Wow, that's like less than two months away. Are you sure you want something that quick?" Nadia asks, being the voice of reason.

"Definitely. It's going to be simple, on a beach with just the Royal Bastards and my dad. I don't need or want anything extravagant. I want to marry Aftermath and make him my husband as soon as possible." I open the Pinterest app on my phone. "Besides I already have the wedding dress picked out, I'm going to ask Jezebelle to cater the food and I want you to be my Maid of Honor."

I show Nadia the dress I have picked out. It's a simple white gown that's strapless and only goes to the middle of my thighs in the front, and long in the back that can wrap around my thighs when needed. I also found a pair of black strappy high-heeled sandals to match. When Nadia doesn't say anything, I turn my attention to her instead of my phone. Her eyes are huge and her mouth is opening and closing like a fish out of water. "What's wrong?"

Matthew's little hand slaps the side of Nadia's face. Good thing he did it so I didn't have to. She shakes her head, her long blonde hair moving with it. "What?" she asks once she snaps out of her stupor.

"What?" I parrot back, confused.

"What did you ask me?" Matthew grabs Nadia's hair and pulls. She gently tugs his hand away.

"I asked you to be my maid of honor. So, will you do it?" I raise an eyebrow and stare at Nadia like she's lost her mind. "Did you hit your head or something?"

Riding Through Life   J. Lynn Lombard

A few patch bunnies come strolling into the kitchen snickering about something, but I don't pay them any attention. Pearl comes in behind them and offers a small smile to Nadia and me. The three of them grab some food and sit down at the island, their backs to us.

"Why would I hit my head?" Nadia asks.

"Cause you're acting weird." I scrunch my nose. "Are you surprised I asked you? If you don't want to do this, I'm not going to be offended."

"I'm shocked that's all. I...I didn't..." Nadia's face turns as red as her Ol' Man's.

"It's OK, Nadia. You don't have to be my maid of honor. I thought we were best friends. I mean," I trail off not wanting to finish this sentence but know I need to. "You're the only female I've been this close to. I've had friends, yes, but nothing like what you and I have."

A tear trails down Nadia's cheek and she wipes it away. "I would be honored to do this with you."

"Yay! I'm so excited!" I squeal jumping up and down. Matthew laughs at his Aunty Kensi acting like a psycho.

"What's going on in here?" Danyella asks as she and Monica enter through the swinging doors.

"I'm getting married!" I shout.

One patch bunny chokes on her food and spins around on her stool. The look of pure hatred crosses her

Riding Through Life   J. Lynn Lombard

face. I don't even remember her name so she isn't relevant to me. Pearl looks genuinely happy for me and my heart soars knowing Pearl, a complete stranger, is happy for me.

"That's so exciting!" Danyella squeals. "Where's the ring? When did he propose?"

"When's the big day?" Monica asks.

"Who's going to be in your wedding?" Danyella pipes in.

"Are you going to do it here at the Clubhouse?" Monica chimes in.

I'm trying to keep track of all their questions. With a smile on my face, I answer them while holding out my left hand. "Aftermath proposed last night, I want a New Year's Eve wedding at the beach with just the Royal Bastards MC, no patch bunnies." I see the smile on Pearl's face drop. "With the exception of one." I wink at her and she drops her head, hiding her beautiful smile so the petty bitches don't notice. "I want my dad there and Nadia is going to be my maid of honor. I don't know who Aftermath is going to ask to be his best man, but I assume it'll be Red."

"A New Year's Eve beach wedding! I absolutely love the idea. Do you have your dress? What about food? Flowers? All the necessities of a wedding? Girl both Monica and I are here to make this the best day of your life." Danyella's excitement is contagious. "Oh! I know, we can have Jezebelle's company cater the food and Daisy can handle the flowers."

Riding Through Life J. Lynn Lombard

"I already have an idea of the dress I want." I pull out my phone and show them.

"Oh, I know where we can get this or one similar." Monica chimes in. If anyone knows anything about shopping, it's Monica. "I will make an appointment to get you in and find your dream dress."

"I want Naomi and Mara Jean as my flower girls and Jaxson as my ring bearer." I chime in.

"Done." Monica sets her phone down. "Our appointment is at one p.m. tomorrow. Do you know what Aftermath and his best man are going to wear?"

My head is spinning with all this information. I'm still wrapping my head around the fact I'm getting married and so much is being planned already.

"Danyella and Monica, quit." Aftermath's deep baritone voice hits me right in the chest. "You're overwhelming my tiger and she's going to claw your eyes out."

I attempt to hold in a laugh at Monica and Danyella gaping at Aftermath but fail miserably. Aftermath wraps me in his arms, kisses the side of my head and then glares at the girls. "The only clawing I'll be doing is to your back." I counter.

A shudder runs through Aftermath's body and he holds me tighter. "Promise?"

"Promise, but later. Right now, the girls are planning our wedding. Do you know who you're going to

Riding Through Life   J. Lynn Lombard

ask to be your best man?" I turn my head so I'm staring into Aftermath's eyes.

"I do, but I still have to ask him."

"So, go do it while we," I point to the ladies with me, "plan our wedding."

Aftermath kisses me one more time before letting me go. "Ok, Tiger, but when I get back..."

"I will claw anything you want." I wink at Aftermath and he growls.

"Not helping, woman." Aftermath leaves the kitchen and the four of us take a seat in the nook nestled in the corner.

Jezebelle, Derange, Torch, Daisy and their kids come into the kitchen. Jezebelle and Daisy head right for us, while Derange and Torch wrangle their kids to eat some breakfast. "What's going on?" Daisy asks.

I hold my left hand out and wiggle my fingers. "I'm getting married and Nadia is my Maid of Honor."

Before I can continue, Danyella chimes in, "We're helping her plan everything. Want to help?"

"Of course we do," Jezebelle answers. She and Daisy take their seats and we plan all the details we can for hours. We eventually move to the common room where there is more room. Jezebelle's son and an RBMC Prospect, Seth, brings us drinks all day long without question. A few times, someone comes up and congratulates me or hugs me. People come and go all day while the six of us plan the best wedding ever.

Riding Through Life   J. Lynn Lombard

    I still can't believe I'm getting married in less than two months. It's surreal that I found the man of my dreams after everything I've been through and we are going to start our lives together. Could anything get better than this?

Riding Through Life   J. Lynn Lombard

Chapter 3

Aftermath

Watching Kensi with the other Ol' Ladies of the Club smiling, laughing and having a good time without a care in the world, makes my black heart skip a beat. They moved from the kitchen to the common room and Seth is bringing them drinks as fast as he can. At this rate, all of them will be three sheets to the wind, except for Nadia. I'm at the bar sipping on a whiskey waiting for Red to get done with his tech shit.

In the beginning, no matter how hard I tried to fight the attraction between us, I couldn't. Despite our age difference, no one in this world has captured my soul the way Kensi did. The woman with her bad history, multi-colored eyes and a spitfire attitude came barreling into my world and turned it upside down.

"What's that goofy grin for?" Red, the Royal Bastards IT guy and my best friend asks as he slaps me on the back. His eyes scan the room for Nadia and his face turns bright red when she spots him. Hence his road name, Red. He blushes at everything and I mean everything. I overheard Nadia and Kensi talking about it one night. No woman I know finds that attractive, but

Riding Through Life   J. Lynn Lombard

Nadia said that is what drew her to him in the first place. Nadia gives him a wink and a smile that lights up her whole face. Will Red be next to tie the knot?

"Just thinking," I answer, sipping on my whiskey. "Want to go for a ride?" I ask. It's now or never. With the way the women are planning everything, we'll be married before I know it.

"Sure. I have to go to Nadia's dance studio and check on the security system. We can swing in there while we're out." Red shrugs his shoulders. Nadia was Red's several night stands and disappeared on him. He went out of his mind trying to locate her and almost lost his patch for it. When he found her, she was being held captive in a stingy abandoned motel by her boss and his sidekick from the strip club, being groomed to be sold on the Black Market. When we got her back, she had a couple of surprises for Red. One, she was pregnant with Red's kid and the other was the two young girls she protected the best she could while pregnant and held captive. Lattimer got away but Josiah is now pig feed by the hands of Nadia, Exleigh and Syvannah.

Once Nadia got her footing here and had Matthew, she opened a dance studio for girls and women who needed a boost to their confidence or a place to escape their everyday hell. Dancing did that for Nadia and with her big heart, she wanted to do the same for others, which is how Royal Dancers formed. Oh, and she is the little sister to who Red calls Nolan-fucking-Ryan, who happens to be dating the most dangerous woman on the West Coast, Krimson, aka Ashley Force.

"Kickstands up in ten," I respond.

Riding Through Life   J. Lynn Lombard

"I only need five." Red shouts over his shoulder as he approaches the ladies. He leans down and gives Nadia a sweltering kiss that leaves her breathless and him blushing. Then he gently kisses Matthew's head and whispers something to them. All the women around swoon and Kensi's gaze lands on me. Her hypnotic eyes capture my attention and I forget where I am and what I'm supposed to be doing.

"Maybe you needed the ten." Red chuckles next to me.

I grunt and rise from my stool, approaching Kensi. I kiss her on the lips which taste like Tequila and seven-up and she grips my hair. I pull away and a whimper leaves Kensi's throat. "I'll be back later. Red and I are going for a ride and stopping at the dance studio."

"Be safe and come back in one piece." The adoration and love shining in my Tiger's eyes swell my black heart.

"You know it, Tiger."

"I love you, Aftermath."

"Love you, too."

I do one of the hardest things I hate doing and that is walking away from my Tiger. I know she is safe and she can take care of herself, but it still makes my chest ache and it feels like a piece of me is missing until we are together again. Kensi has been through so much

Riding Through Life   J. Lynn Lombard

in her young life that, if there's something I can do to make it better for her, you bet your ass I will.

    Red and I mount our bikes and ride out of the garage. Bones and a Prospect, who is Daisy's twin, Knight, are manning the rolling gate. Once they spot us, the buzzer sounds and the chain link fence rolls to the right, giving us room to exit. Back a couple of years ago, the Mexican Cartel tried to overtake our Clubhouse. They smashed the gates, came in guns blazing and killed one of our prospects, Alex. He was young, homeless, a good kid trying to survive in a fucked up world. Derange found him and brought him in as a hang-around for a while until he was old enough to prospect. He was close to earning his colors until he wasn't. It still angers me to this day how someone could be so cruel to a young man trying to find his way. If we didn't take out Salazar, I'm sure none of us would be here right now breathing the salty air in our lungs.

    We take a detour and ride south along the coast, letting the chilly air nip our exposed skin while the cloudy sky keeps us from being sunburnt. I find a parking lot that looks over the ocean and signal for us to enter. Even though it's cloudy today, the sun is still trying to peek through and tease us with her warmth. Red pulls up next to me and pulls his gaiter down.

    "Everything OK, Aftermath?"

    I turn off the engine and unbuckle my brain bucket. Leaning on the handlebars of my Harley Davidson Ultra Street Glide, I stare out into the ocean, watching the waves change the sand with every splash. Kind of like my life. One moment I was set in my ways

Riding Through Life   J. Lynn Lombard
and the next, a whisp of a woman turned my world on its head. "Let's walk."

I climb off my bike and Red does the same. Together we walk down the beach until the water laps at our boots. Standing there, I stare out into the ocean, letting the noises drown out my thoughts.

Scrubbing a hand down my face, my beard rough against my palms, I blow out a deep breath. "As you know, I asked Kensi to marry me." Red stands next to me awkwardly but doesn't say anything, waiting for me to continue. My heart is beating hard in my chest and my hands shake. I don't have a fucking clue why I'm so nervous. "I don't have much in the form of a family except for this club and my mom. I consider you to be my closest friend." Jesus, why does this have to be so fucking hard?

"What I'm asking, Red is, willyoubemybestman?" I rush the words together afraid if I say them slowly, lightning will strike me dead for some reason.

Red stands next to me completely mute. I turn my head in his direction when he doesn't answer me and the little fucker has a shit-eating grin on his face. "Fuck dude, you made it sound like you were having your teeth pulled with no Novocaine." He shakes his head, "Of course, I'll be your best man. I'll be the bestest best man anyone has ever heard of."

"What the fuck is a bestest best man?" I mutter.

Riding Through Life   J. Lynn Lombard

Red shrugs his shoulders, his face turning red from embarrassment. "No fucking idea. It sounded better in my head than it did out loud. Now that that worst best man proposal is done, are you ready to head to the dance studio? The sooner we get that done, the quicker we can get back to the Clubhouse."

I shove Red and head back for my bike. "Don't be a fucker, dick. I've never had to do that before."

Red catches up with a smirk on his face. "None of us have ever had to do any of this before and I have a feeling things will get harder before we get any peace."

I groan, "Fuck, dude. Why'd you say that? Now you jinxed me."

Red shakes his head, "Nah, I'm just stating the obvious. When shit is going good and all is quiet, something is bound to happen to stir up shit." He straps his helmet on and I do the same. We fire up our bikes and head toward Nadia's dance studio.

Riding Through LifeJ. Lynn Lombard

Chapter 4

Aftermath

Red slows down and turns left onto a quiet street. Nadia's dance studio sits on the right, standing out in the open for anyone to see. The soft grey brick with black trim is warm and inviting. In the center of the building is a big neon sign in blue that reads Royal Dancers. Our club logo is on the bottom right. The parking lot is freshly paved with streetlights every ten feet or so, that way the customers feel safe leaving here no matter what time of day or night it is. The point of this location, according to Nadia, is it's open and inviting for teenagers and adults to come in and learn to dance.

We park our bikes near the huge glass doors and dismount. I remove my brain bucket and set it on the seat. Then, I pull the gaiter down from my face and take off my leather gloves stuffing them in the pocket of my cut. We might be in California, but during the fall months, Mother Nature is a fickle bitch. It's about 60 degrees today and when you're riding it's a lot fucking colder.

Riding Through Life   J. Lynn Lombard

Taking in my surroundings, I see multiple cars parked close to the building. "Business is doing good, isn't it?" I ask.

Red nods his head. "Yeah. Nadia hired a new dance instructor to help pick up the slack and bring in more classes. I guess they used to work together at a strip club and Nadia said this woman is trustworthy. I ran her background and so far everything is on the up and up but just because something isn't out there, doesn't mean they're a good person."

"What's up, Red?" I ask stopping our forward progress into the studio.

Red releases a deep sigh and runs his hands down his face. Since he started wearing his contacts, he looks different but good. "I don't know. This new instructor rubs me the wrong way, which is why I'm here tightening security rather than at home with my Ol' Lady and kid."

I slap my hands together, making a loud cracking noise. "Then let's get this shit done and get back to our women."

We walk into the entrance of the dance studio. There is a reception desk directly in front of us with no one manning it since it's Saturday afternoon. We walk across the foyer on the soft grey wall to wall carpet leading to the back of the building where the lights are on. The closer we walk, the louder the dance music filters down the hallway. I follow Red as we step inside the spacious room. The room has mirrors with a gold bar thingy running in the middle of them against the walls

Riding Through Life   J. Lynn Lombard

and hardwood flooring. The eight women stop dancing and turn to stare at us as we enter.

Red continues to walk along the edge of the hardwood floor ignoring the women in here. I keep an eye on them as I follow behind Red. A woman wearing tight black leggings with a black tank top and white shoes stands in front of the room. Her hair is up in a messy bun thingy and her blue eyes follow our movement. When my gaze lifts and collide with hers, she winks at me and gives her hips an extra sway. Totally obvious what she's doing, I give her a deadly glare, making sure she knows I'm not interested. What the fuck was that?

Red and I enter the room at the back of the studio and he takes a seat at the table where the monitors are set up. He turns each camera on one by one until all nine of them show every inch of this place. "That was intense." Red mumbles, his face turning red. "Do you see what I mean about her?"

I shiver, remembering how her eyes tracked my every movement. "That was creepy as fuck." I take a seat and watch Red do whatever it is he does.

After a while, I grow bored. "I'm going to go for a walk and check the perimeters. It appears all the dancers are gone now." I say standing up.

Red grunts his acknowledgement and I leave the security room. The dance room lights are turned down low and I cross the hardwood floor, my boots echoing around me. I open the door and enter the carpeted

Riding Through Life   J. Lynn Lombard

hallway. The lights are turned down here too and I carefully make my way to the front of the studio.

Turning left, I enter another dimly lit hallway. Two doors are on my left, one on my right and a big bay window is in front of me. The one on my right is Nadia's office and the other two on my left lead to male and female locker rooms. I check Nadia's office door and it's locked tight. I walk down the end of the hallway and make sure the window is shut and locked.

Turning around, I check the men's locker room door and it's locked tight. My hand rests on the women's locker room and an eerie feeling crawls up my spine. I knock before pushing on the door, surprised it gives way, opening for me.

"Hello?" I call out. I wait for a beat before I take a small step inside. My heart is hammering in my chest. Something is off and I don't like it. "Hello? Is anyone in here?"

The locker room is silent and I step further inside. It's clean with standard blue lockers taking up three rows and a bench in between each row. My boots echo off the concrete floor as I walk further inside, cringing from the sound. If someone is here, then they definitely know I'm here.

To the far back are four stand-up shower stalls and to the right at the back are four bathroom stalls. I check each stall for someone in here. When there is no sign of anyone, I turn to leave. Making my way back to the front of the locker room I sit down on the bench and take a breath, wiping the nervous sweat from my brow.

Riding Through Life   J. Lynn Lombard

I've been a ball of nerves since I walked in here and I don't know why. I've been around stripper rooms my whole life and have seen many, many women shake their goods to earn a living. I don't know why I'm freaking out.

A small, warm hand wraps around my bicep. The scent of perfume floats into my nose. A low sultry voice purrs against my ear, making my skin crawl. "Are you looking for me?" The woman presses her chest against my back.

"Get your fucking hands off me." I ground out through clenched teeth.

The woman tsks and I turn my head. I notice the new dance instructor hovering over my back, invading my space. She takes a step back, naked as the day she was born, her ample chest proudly on display, her flat toned stomach quivers in anticipation and the landing strip leading to her lady bits is the same blonde as her hair. Her bright blue eyes are dark with desire. "Did I snag myself a Royal Bastard?" She breathes heavily.

I stand up quickly before this woman can throw herself at me and leave the locker room. Holy shit. What the hell was that all about?

I hurry to my bike and send a text to Red.

Riding Through Life					J. Lynn Lombard

Riding Through Life   J. Lynn Lombard

Chapter 5

Aftermath

It's been a few days since that bitch came on to me and I haven't told Kensi about it. The guilt is eating away at me, but nothing happened so why should I worry her when there isn't anything to worry about?

Torch, Daisy, Derange and Jezebelle are playing pool, while Nadia with Matthew, Monica, Kensi and Danyella are working on wedding shit on the large dining room table. Capone, Blayze, Trigger and Dagger are playing darts, while Tiny with his new kitten, Peanut, are sitting with some bunnies on the couch. Syvannah and Exleigh are holed up in their room. They're taking the trauma they endured day by day. Some days are good and some days are bad. The Prospects Seth and Knight are tending bar, while Bones and Pretty Boy are sitting at the gates. Seth and Knight will be heading out there in a little while to relieve Bones and Pretty Boy. The only person missing right now is Red, who's cooped up in his communications room searching for Lattimer, Rose and Jax, Torch's twin brother and wife, I think. Everyone is laughing, talking, listening to music and having a good time. It's been a while since everyone has been relaxed

Riding Through Life   J. Lynn Lombard

and I take it all in while sitting at the bar drinking a beer. My eyes connect with Kensi and she offers me a secret smile that tells me I'm going to be up for a long night, in more ways than one.

Once the game of darts is over, Capone whistles, quieting the chatter down. "We need a store run," Capone shouts. I duck my head, hoping he doesn't notice me. I fucking hate store runs. Being cooped up in a cage with two patch bunnies is not my idea of fun. "Thanks for volunteering, Aftermath. Take Pearl and Lexi with you. They have the list of shit we need."

I grumble but nod my head, "Aye, Prez." Pearl is a good woman but I think she is hiding from something or someone. The last time we had a bunny hide in our Clubhouse, Torch found his twin he didn't know about, Jax.

Pearl climbs off Tiny's lap and sways her hips towards me. If I didn't get to know Pearl, I'd think she was trying to tempt me, but she isn't. It's just the way she walks. Like sexy confidence is bred into her and it's a natural thing for her. "I'll get Lexi and then we can leave." The rasp of Pearl's voice breaks through my thoughts.

"I'll be right here." I give her a quick smile, but not anything to where she'd think I was hitting on her. That's not me and never will be.

"We should be ready in like ten minutes." Pearl acknowledges and saunters off to the back of the Clubhouse where the Patch Bunnies stay. Kensi smirks before returning her attention to what Danyella is saying. The little minx is going to pay for that later. I

Riding Through Life   J. Lynn Lombard

swallow the last of my beer and rise from the stool when Pearl and Lexi come out of their room. They head for the garage and I take a detour toward Kensi. Turning her chair around, I lean over Kensi, getting an eyeful of her cleavage while boxing her in her chair. Our lips are a breath apart when Kensi darts her pink tongue out to lick hers, driving me insane.

"I'll be back in a few." I lean my forehead against hers and block out all the other noises around us. It's just Kensi and me.

"Be safe," she whispers against my lips causing my body to quiver with want, lust and love for this woman. She is the only person in my life who cares about my safety except for my mom and the Royal Bastards. My heart pounds against my chest as it swells for the love I have for this woman.

"You know I will." I kiss Kensi roughly, claiming her as mine and mine alone. When I pull away and look around, all the women's eyes are on us shining with adoration. Kensi giggles, her multi-colored eyes lighting up with mischief. "Stay out of trouble while I'm gone."

"You know I'll try," she counters. I kiss her again and walk away before I can't.

The trip to the grocery store was uneventful. Lexi sat in the back of the Club's cage while Pearl sat up front. Both women have their hair fixed to perfection, their makeup flawless and they're both wearing RBMC t-shirts with black leggings. They know when they're out

Riding Through Life   J. Lynn Lombard

in public, no matter what they choose to do behind their doors, they are to represent us with the highest regard.

Pulling into a parking spot, I shut the SUV off and climb out. Lexi and Pearl do the same. I scan our surroundings making sure it's safe for the two women while we head inside.

"I'll grab a cart." Pearl offers but I shake her off. Even though I hate grocery runs, I won't be a dick and make them push the cart.

"I got it. You ladies get what we need and I'll follow." I grab a cart from the corral and wouldn't it be my fucking luck, the wheel is busted. Pearl giggles, covering her mouth with the palm of her hand while Lexi smirks. These two are completely opposite, but they make their friendship work. While Pearl is tall and slender with long, straight, light blonde, almost white hair and skin so light, you'd think she was an albino, Lexi is the complete opposite. She's short, maybe pushing five foot two, with dark sun-kissed skin, long onyx curls, a full-figured woman with curves in all the right places.

Pearl sways her hips while she walks and looks items over very carefully before placing them in the cart, while Lexi grabs shit off the shelf and doesn't give a fuck what it is or how much it costs. She hates shopping just as much as I do.

We're almost finished and I'm fidgeting with my squeaky cart that's getting on my last nerve when we turn down the last aisle and I almost run into someone. "Oh, sorry," I grunt without looking up.

Riding Through Life   J. Lynn Lombard

A giggle escapes the woman, "No worries Mr. Biker Man, it seems we keep on running into each other." The seductive voice makes my head snap up. Pearl and Lexi stop what they're doing and watch the woman with hate-filled eyes. "Only this time, I'm wearing clothes." She shrugs her shoulders and saunters away not waiting for my response. "That sucks for me this time, 'cause I remember last time *real well*." She calls over her shoulder and before I can respond and call her a liar, the blonde woman is gone.

"What the fuck was that?" Pearl asks, settling her hands on her hips. She looks like she wants to throw down and it won't matter if it's me or someone else.

"Not your business." I grit out through clenched teeth. "Are we fucking done yet?" I growl.

"Whatever." Pearl rolls her eyes and places the last item in our cart.

The three of us don't speak a word while we check out and head to the cage. I'm still fighting the broken tire, making my mood turn pissy. Pearl and Lexi get into the SUV, neither one talking to me but sure are giving me death glares. Once I have all the groceries loaded into the back, I slam the trunk down. My mood went from bad to worse when the squeaky tire decides to be a little fucker and I don't look where I'm going.

A warm body presses against my side and a slight purr wraps around me. "I'll see you later, Biker."

And yet again the woman takes off before I can shake myself out of the idiot I've become. I slam the cart

Riding Through Life   J. Lynn Lombard

into the cart parking and stomp to the SUV. I climb inside and slam the door so hard, it rocks the SUV.

"Not a fucking word to anyone. Do you hear me?" I bark as I start the cage and drive away. Now what the fuck am I going to do? Not tell Kensi that's what. Nothing happened so there is nothing to tell.

Riding Through Life   J. Lynn Lombard

Chapter 6

Aftermath

It's been a week and Lexi and Pearl haven't said a word to anyone. Thank fuck for small favors. Guilt and embarrassment have been eating away at me but I know if I tell Kensi, it'll send her into a tailspin. Nothing happened, so why do I feel so guilty?

"What's up, brother?" Red asks as he sits at the barstool next to me. Kensi is at her dad's house in Cannondale Springs and I'm here drinking whiskey trying to drink away my problem. I've been pissy all week, waiting for the shoe to drop, but it hasn't and I can't keep going on like this.

"Nothing." I slam another shot down and don't feel the burn anymore. My eyes are glossy and my vision blurs. Shit, I'm fucked up.

"Bullshit. You've been acting weird ever since you went with me to Nadia's dance studio. Did something happen that you didn't tell me about?" I grunt out a no and Red's eyes grow wide like he figured it out, which he probably has since he's smart as fuck. "Fuck."

Riding Through Life   J. Lynn Lombard

"Yeah, fuck." I swallow another shot and slam the shot glass on the bar top. Knight scurries over and grabs my glass, putting it away. "Hey, I wasn't done with that." I'm angry this little fucker thinks he can take away my drink. I'll show him.

I lean over the bar top and attempt to grab Knight and show him who's in charge when I miss and before I can topple over, a strong grip pulls me back onto my seat and I topple ass over tea kettle in the other direction making my head spin. I can't stop myself in this state, so I brace for impact. All my drunken weight lands on my right shoulder when I hit the ground with a hard thunk. I cut an icy glare to Red, but he's holding his hands up in the air. "What the fuck?!" I shout, ready to kick some ass. I struggle to stand up when a boot lands on my chest, stopping me.

"Watch yourself, Aftermath." Capone stands over me and I exhale a deep breath. Fuck.

"Fuck is right." Capone leans down and gets in my face. His deadly black eyes pin me to my spot. "My daughter is here, Aftermath. If you want to get shit-faced drunk, then do it in your room, not out here where young, impressionable girls are roaming around."

I swallow hard and nod, my heart is hammering against my chest at a frenzied pace. "Sorry, Prez. It won't happen again."

"You're fucking right it won't happen again." He offers his hand to help me up and I take it. That's the one thing about this brotherhood. You can fuck up, get your ass handed to you and then be forgiven in less than thirty seconds. "Church in ten. Sober your ass up and quickly."

Capone walks away with Blayze and I scowl. "What are you going to do?" Red asks.

"About what?" I look at him wrinkling my forehead.

"About your problem."

"I don't have a fucking problem because nothing fucking happened," I counter. If I keep telling myself this, it should come true. I didn't do anything wrong. Once I saw that woman was naked, I high tailed it out of Nadia's dance studio and haven't been back since. "Nothing happened so there's nothing to tell."

Red shakes his head and hands me a cup of coffee. "Word of advice?"

"Sure, this'll be interesting." I pay attention to Red while sipping my coffee, trying to sober up for Church.

His face burns bright red, like his name. "I believe you if nothing happened, but something did happen and if you don't tell Kensi about it, shit will get worse and you'll break her trust, even if *you* didn't do anything."

Fuck. Red's right. I release a deep sigh and take another swallow of my coffee. "Fine. I'll tell her and hope she doesn't go all Harley Quinn on my ass. Even though that outfit would look sexy as hell on her." I'm sober now but drunk on images of Kensi in booty shorts

Riding Through Life   J. Lynn Lombard

with black ripped stockings, black combat boots, a baby doll t-shirt, and her hair up in pigtails while carrying around a baseball bat and blowing bubbles. I shiver and shake the image away knowing if I go into Church with a hard-on the guys will rib me forever.

Red and I enter Church with Torch, Dagger, Tiny, Pretty Boy and Bones. Capone, Blayde and Derange are already inside. Their faces are impassive as they look up from the paperwork spread out on the scarred table. Whatever this is isn't going to be good. The three of them remain silent as we take our respective seats. Red pulls out his laptop and sets it on the table, turning it on. He's not only our IT guy, but he's our secretary too. He takes impeccable notes for every meeting. It's been discussed for either Bones or Pretty Boy to take over as Secretary, but Red hasn't wanted to give it up yet. Said he doesn't know which brother will take notes the way he does.

Capone lights up a cigarette, exhales the smoke and slams his ivory gavel onto the scarred table signaling Church to begin. "Our contact reached out to us asking for our help, again. He said his clients were so impressed with our last job that he has more lined up if we want them." Capone takes another drag off his cigarette before putting it out and continuing. "That means if this pans out, they will be paying us twice as much as the guns and drugs we're running through the Cartel. We can finally break away from them."

Hoots and hollers along with fists banging on the table celebrate Capone's news. We've been trying to find a way out of the Cartel's clutches for the past two years and hopefully, this is it.

Riding Through Life   J. Lynn Lombard

Capone holds up his hands, silencing the room. "This is a perfect shift for our Club. This way we don't have to use the Casino as much as we do now. Only for the underground fighting rings. But it's going to take time. We have to set up a new buyer, a new runner and get the Cartel on board with them. All in favor of taking this on and moving away from the guns and drugs say aye."

Each member starting with Bones and Pretty Boy agrees with this change. Capone slams his gavel on the table, "It's unanimous. Torch and Aftermath, reach out to your contacts and get a feel for who wants to take over for us. If anyone else has a contact they trust, run it by Red and he'll get the background check done to see if they are a fit."

We're all watching as Red types furiously on his laptop as Capone speaks. Once Red is done, he lifts his head and looks around the room. Noticing all eyes are on him, his face flushes a deep shade of red and flips everyone off grumbling under his breath about assholes and dickheads.

"Ok, next order of business, Derange, go ahead." Capone signals for Derange to take the floor. He shuffles the papers that were sprawled out on the table and hands each of us a copy. On it is a young girl around eighteen years old with her whole life ahead of her. She's smiling into the camera like she has a secret that everyone wants to know about but no one does. Her blue eyes are sparkling with mischief and her blonde hair is styled to perfection without a hair out of place.

Riding Through Life   J. Lynn Lombard

"Our contact got in touch with me. Three weeks ago, this girl named Denise Athens disappeared. She was last seen at a high school party and never came home. Her parents contacted the local PD and they are hitting a brick wall with this one. Denise's clothes were found dirty and caked with blood about five miles from the party on a desolate dirt road. Her car was found in a ravine, covered with rocks and debris and had blood splatters on the windshield and steering wheel but was wiped clean of any prints or fibers. No tire tracks showing she skidded off the road or tried to stop. They're at a loss on what to do and that's why they contacted us." Derange looks at me before speaking next. "Sherriff Donovan thinks this has to do with the Black Market Railroad and is asking for our help."

Shit. Kensi's dad, my future father-in-law, is our contact for Capone? Has he been feeding us these jobs when his hands are tied knowing we can and will get it done? Does Kensi know about this? Does Donovan know what we do to these types of people? Is he setting us up?

"Aftermath, I can see the wheels spinning, brother. What's going on inside that big head of yours?" Capone asks, cool, calm and collected while I'm feeling anything but.

"How do we know this is legit? Does he know what we do to pigs like these?" I question.

"Of course, he does and he has known since you started dating his daughter and brought him into the Clubhouse." Capone leans forward and steeples his hands together like a prayer. "I didn't tell you who our contact was until I knew for sure your relationship with Kensi was the real deal. Her dad is walking a thin line between right and wrong and Kensi doesn't know anything about it. She's been in the dark this whole time and it's going to stay that way. Are we clear?"

"Crystal clear." I nod my head, turning all this information over in my brain. Another secret I'm keeping from Kensi. Fuck. My future father-in-law has been hiring us to do search and rescue missions this whole time, knowing what we do with the men we find and to top it off, he is an ex-FBI agent and now a Sheriff. What the actual fuck?

"Good, we need to tread lightly with this. There are big players involved and I don't know how deep their connections go. One is a Sheriff from a neighboring county and that's how this was brought to Donovan's attention. These are the men going out on this trip and trying to find this young lady. I need the best of the best for this job so that is Aftermath, Trigger, Tiny and Pretty Boy. Use your resources to make people talk, I don't care what you have to do to get the job done. You'll roll out tomorrow morning." Capone slams his gavel on the table ending this discussion.

"Does anyone else have anything they want to bring up today?" Capone asks.

Bones raises his hand, "I do, Prez."

Capone nods, "Go for it."

"I'd like to open a Gentleman's club. One ran by us and we only hire the best dancers who aren't strung out on drugs. Who will work for us, not because they have to but because they want to." Bones hesitates before adding, "And if it's agreed upon, I would like Silver Grace to manage them. She has a lot of experience in this line of work and women trust her."

My gaze flies to Bones, accessing him. Is he crushing on my mom? Do I have to kick his ass? He's twenty years younger than she is! My nostrils flare the more I think about Bones chasing after my mother.

"It's not what you think, Aftermath." Bones disputes quickly.

"Tell me what I'm fucking thinking, Bones," I growl low and deep. If he says one wrong word, he will be a limp pile of bones because I will beat him within an inch of his life.

"She is a beautiful woman." Bones states. I'm close to losing it so I growl. "She knows what to look for in a dancer and how to successfully run a business like this. I'm not recommending her for the job because I have a teenage fantasy for a MILF. She needs something to do and I thought this would be perfect for her." Bones argues his case. "She's not happy sitting around not doing anything. I swear, Brother, this is not a sexual fantasy of mine."

"Is my mom not good enough for your spank bank?" I interject.

"What the fuck, Aftermath?" Trigger chuckles. I drag my deadly gaze from Bones to Trigger. "You're pissed if he does have a MILF issue and you're pissed if he doesn't. Make up your fucking mind. You sound like a hormonal woman."

"I am not a hormonal woman!" I slam my fist onto the table, making the steady oak shake. "I don't want one of my brothers fucking my mother! She is off limits!"

"No one is fucking your mom in this Clubhouse, Aftermath. Pull your shit together." Red hisses in my ear.

I narrow my gaze at Red and he holds steady. He doesn't cower like most men do. "Get a grip, brother. You're seeing something that isn't there."

I shift my gaze back to Bones. "Is this true? You aren't fucking my mom?"

Bones shakes his head, "Fuck no, Aftermath. She's like a mom to me. Even though she's hot as fuck, I'd never mess around with her."

Huh, maybe I had all this wrong. I lean back in my seat and cross my arms over my chest.

"Are we done with the pissing contest?" Capone asks raising an eyebrow. I nod my head and don't say a word. I really need to pull my shit together like Red keeps telling me. "Bones, I want the cost of everything for this project. From the building to the dancers, down to how much paint will cost. Get with Trigger and crunch some numbers. If it looks good, bring it to vote at the next meeting." Capone slams his gavel on the table. "Meeting adjourned."

Riding Through Life   J. Lynn Lombard

Everyone stands up to leave except Red, Capone and Blayze. I raise an eyebrow but Red shakes his head. He can't tell me what is going on yet. I have to trust that if he needs us, he will let us know. I leave the Chapel following Bones and Trigger talking about the club Bones wants to open. It does sound like a great idea, but I still don't like my mom running it.

I'm grumpy as fuck as I take a seat at the bar waiting for Kensi to get back from her dad's. A familiar giggle pierces my ears and my stomach drops to my feet. I turn my head and the busty blonde from Nadia's dance studio is playing pool with Knight, staring at me.

I grab a bottle from behind the bar and hightail it to my room. There is no fucking way I'm staying out there without Kensi. Fuck that. If I have to leave in the morning, the last thing I want to do is fight with my Ol' Lady over some bitch.

Chapter 7

Kensi

"Oh, shit." I groan as Aftermath slams into me, hitting all the right spots. "Harder, Mark." I moan as he drives into me. Sweat coats our bodies and my breathing is short and rapid. Aftermath licks and nips at the skin connecting my neck and ear and I detonate around him. Aftermath drives forward one more time, swelling inside of me as he bites the column of my neck. He empties himself inside of me. I'm a limp noodle when Aftermath pulls his softening shaft from my body and I shiver.

"Wow." That's all I can say when I stretch my body like a cat and rest my head on his chest. Aftermath's heart is beating hard against my ear and his breathing is short and rapid.

"I love you, Kensi Donovan. Soon to be Mrs. Kensi Jacobs." Aftermath kisses the top of my head.

"I love you too, Mark Jacobs, my soon-to-be husband." My lips linger on Aftermath's chiseled chest and he grunts happily in response.

"Keep that up woman and round three will start any moment." Aftermath threatens and it turns me on.

Riding Through Life
J. Lynn Lombard

"I need a bath first. My lady bits are sore from the last few days." I pout.

Aftermath has been very attentive for the last week and I am not complaining. I'm not sure what is going on inside his head, but if he wants to give me multiple orgasms in a day, I'm down for it. I trust him with my whole being and if it's something I need to know, Aftermath will tell me. Otherwise, I'll keep my mouth shut and my brain from working overtime and enjoy these multiple orgasms a day.

"With as much as I'd love to sink into you again, Tiger. You have to go to your dad's house and if you're late and smell like sex, he is really going to shoot my ass." Aftermath swats my naked ass getting me to move off his chest.

I rise from our bed and saunter toward the en-suite bathroom. I glance at Aftermath over my shoulder, giving him my backside, which I know he loves and my best come hither look. "Fine. You can join me in the shower. We can get dirty before we get clean."

Aftermath grunts before leaping off the bed and caging me against the wall. "What am I going to do with you, woman?" His lips are on my neck and my legs shake with anticipation.

"You can do whatever you want with me," I respond breathlessly. Aftermath picks me up and I wrap my legs around his waist. I slowly sink onto his growing erection as he stumbles his way into the bathroom. Moaning, I take him as deep as I can from this angle and work myself up and down his length. Aftermath starts the shower and carefully steps under the warm spray.

Riding Through Life   J. Lynn Lombard

We make love two more times before we get out and I leave to see my dad.

I'm driving my new Dodge Durango, Aftermath swore I needed, up the 401 on my way to see my dad. He is the Sheriff of a neighboring county and since he works weird hours, I decided to go to his house instead of him coming to the Clubhouse. I've done this drive a few times a week to see my dad since he moved up here and usually Aftermath is with me, but today he had club business to take care of. Only the Royal Bastard members know what that business entails and we Ol' ladies are left in the dark. Or so they think. Danyella and Jezebelle can make their men sing like canaries when they really want to. I, on the other hand, sing like a canary when Aftermath gives me his sexy smirk.

I get off at the exit that leads to Cannondale Springs and take a left. I notice a dark blue SUV in my rearview mirror following a few car lengths back that exits the same time I do. I narrow my eyes and pick up speed. The dark blue SUV does the same. Motherfuckers. Is this seriously happening right now?

I take a sharp left onto a dirt road and take another right as soon as I can. Desert sand is kicking up behind me when I make a full circle back onto the pavement. I think I lost them as I hurry down to the quiet neighborhood and park my Durango behind my dad's house and turn off the engine. My heart is hammering hard against my chest and I feel like I'm going to be sick.

Riding Through Life   J. Lynn Lombard

Those motherfuckers better not be who I think they are and mess with me or my dad. We're both finally in a good place and the last thing we need is the fucking G-men to fuck up our lives again.

A knock on my window scares the crap out of me. "Holy shit!" I rest my palm on my chest, trying to calm my heart which is slamming against my ribs. "Are you trying to give me a heart attack?"

My dad stands next to the door with his hands on his hips and a raised brow graces his handsome features. He is wearing a pair of dark blue jeans, a black t-shirt that hugs his muscles, a baseball hat on backward and his no bullshit attitude. My dad is definitely a DILF with his tall and lean stature, salt and pepper hair, toned muscles for a man in his fifties and a smoking hot California tan. I don't know why no one has snagged him up yet. I snort to myself, yeah I do know why. After my mom left and took my little brother, my dad has had major trust issues. "You OK, Lil' Kay?"

I open the door and step outside. The air is crisp for late October and it stings my lungs. "Yeah, I'm OK, Dad." Closing and locking my Durango, I peek around him and breathe a sigh of relief when I don't see the dark SUV rolling by.

"Come on inside. I've made your favorite for lunch." Dad smiles and shows off his straight, pearly white teeth. He knows something is up but won't say anything until I do.

"Grilled cheese and tomato soup?" I ask with excitement in my voice. It's been so long since I've had this childhood staple.

Riding Through Life   J. Lynn Lombard

"With extra cheese," Dad smirks.

"What are we waiting for?" I loop my arm around his and we walk up the back porch together.

Dad releases my arm and opens the door. I step in before him and the smell of buttered bread, cheese and tomatoes assaults my nose before I even make it through the back mudroom. My stomach growls in anticipation.

Dad removes his running shoes while chuckling and enters the kitchen. I toe off my shoes and follow him in my stocking feet. His kitchen is to die for. The one at the Clubhouse is high tech and huge, but Dad's is small with all the latest appliances. A stainless steel refrigerator is nestled into the wall to make more space. The stove and dishwasher match the refrigerator on the opposite wall. There is a small window above the kitchen sink and a nook in the opposite corner with a big bay window, facing the rising sun. Black with swirls of green granite countertops are spread out throughout the kitchen with a matching island.

I sit down on one of the black stools surrounding the island and prop my elbows on it. Dad pulls down two white plates and two white bowls. After he dishes out the soup and puts two pieces of grilled cheese on the adjacent plate, he brings them over to me.

"Do you want water, milk or tea?"

"Water, please."

Riding Through Life   J. Lynn Lombard

Soon we are both enjoying our lunch and making small talk. Once the food is gone and the dishes are put in the dishwasher, we move into the living room.

Dad sits in his recliner next to the big windows that overlook the street. I take a seat on the fluffy grey couch. "Man, this couch is phenomenal. I need to get one of these when our house is done." I groan, stretching. "I could use a nap now. I'm in a food coma." I yawn.

Dad chuckles but something is wrong. I can see it in his eyes. "What's wrong?" I ask on high alert. My mind goes back to the dark SUV following me here.

"What makes you say that Lil' Kay?" He averts his eyes to look out the window.

I roll mine. "Dad, I know you. I know you're hiding something or it has you spooked."

"So, what did you have to tell me?" Instead of answering me, he changes the subject. Stubborn man. I want to stomp my foot but I know it won't do any good.

If that's the game he wants to play then fine. I'll make him choke on his thoughts for a little bit. "Mark and I are getting married on New Year's Eve."

Dad's head whips in my direction. His eyes are wide and his mouth is opening and closing like a fish out of water. "That's… That's…"

"Like less than two months away?" I finish for him. He nods his head. "I know but I don't want to wait any longer. The Ol' Ladies and I have everything already planned out. It's going to be on the beach with our family there. I don't want nor need anything huge. The club and you are all who I want to witness this next step in my life."

Dad's eyes meet mine and a small smile spreads across his face. "Can I... can I have the honor of walking you down the aisle?"

I rise from the couch and walk over to Dad sitting in the chair. I squat down and lean on his legs like I used to do when I was a little girl. Tears are swimming in his precious gaze as he stares down at me. "Of course, you can, Daddy. I would be honored to have you give me away to Mark." He wraps his strong arms around me and hugs me tight. I'm a blubbering mess by the time we let go of each other.

"You've just made me the happiest father in the world, Lil' Kay." He brushes the tears off my cheeks.

"You're the best dad ever. I'm sorry for everything I put you through." Dad hugs me tight and I feel his body shuddering against mine.

Dad pulls back and cups my cheeks in his big strong hands. "I'm sorry too, Lil' Kay. I'm sorry I didn't believe you when you told me about your friend. I'm sorry I didn't try hard enough when the Bureau wouldn't help me look for you. And I'm sorry I failed as a father to the most precious child in the world."

My stomach sinks to my toes when Dad brings up the FBI and his old job. "Dad?" I croak.

"Yeah, Lil' Kay?"

Riding Through Life   J. Lynn Lombard

    I turn my head to stare out the big living room windows. Across the street is the dark SUV that was tailing me earlier. The doors open and four men in dark suits exit, staring at the house like they can make it disappear or burn down with us inside. "I think we have an issue."

Riding Through Life   J. Lynn Lombard

Chapter 8

Kensi

Getting out of my dad's house was not an easy task, but I managed to leave without issue or being tailed. Which was a big relief. The last thing I need or want are the G-men following me around and causing trouble with the club. I already get myself into enough trouble as it is.

I pull through the gates being manned by Bones and Knight and I wonder where Pretty Boy is. Usually, he and Bones are paired off together. Oh well, not my concern. I park my Durango in a parking spot and notice a few extra cars in the lot. One is a light blue bug, a grey Saturn, a black Charger and a white Focus, all girly cars. No one told me there was a party tonight. After the day I had, the last thing I want to do is socialize. I hope Aftermath isn't down for it tonight, because I know I can't handle it and will either get myself into trouble or get arrested. Neither sounds appealing to me right now.

Releasing a deep breath, I turn off my Durango and climb out. Locking the doors behind me, I pocket my keys and head inside. I open the side door and walk

Riding Through Life J. Lynn Lombard

down the corridor that leads into the Clubhouse. The further I walk, the louder the music is.

Entering the common room, the first thing I notice is a busty blonde dancing on the pool table. Her long blonde hair is plastered to her forehead from sweating and she isn't hiding the goods her mama gave her. She swings and juts her hips like she was born to dance like this. Good lord, help me now. She has all the single men's eyes on her and Playboy is getting into her moves.

Nadia notices me walking in and she is by my side in an instant. Soon enough the other Ol' Ladies are gathered around me with their men and some of the other brothers from the Club. Each brother is hugging me, including Playboy, telling me they're glad I'm back. I don't see Aftermath anywhere but that isn't anything that worries me. When it gets rowdy, Aftermath likes to disappear and stay away. What worries me is the blonde dancing on the pool table. She does some spin moves and shouts. She would be a beauty to watch if I didn't notice the look of disdain on her face when she noticed me. Her body moves harder and faster like she is trying to impress everyone and gain attention back on her. When she can't get the attention back on her, she jumps off the table and struts off down the hallway toward our rooms.

"Do you know her?" I ask Nadia.

Nadia rolls her eyes and huffs, "Yeah, I do, and right now I'm regretting bringing her here. She's one of my new dancers and doesn't have a lot of friends. I thought if she came here, she would be able to let loose and relax, but something about her is setting my radar off." Nadia explains.

I look in the direction of where she is going and follow her. At least it isn't only me who thinks something is up with this chick. Quieting my footsteps, I creep down the hallway that leads to our rooms and the bunny's rooms. Before I can find her, big strong arms wrap around my waist and Aftermath's lips are on my neck.

He inhales before kissing the spot where my neck and shoulder meet, "Hmmm, I've missed you."

"I missed you too," I groan, enjoying Aftermath's touch. I turn in his arms and he picks me up, pressing my back against the wall. A light scent of perfume invades my nose and I freeze. I peer over Aftermath's shoulder and see the woman lingering in the hallway. I open my mouth to tell this Peeping Tom off but Aftermath's lips are back on mine while he carries us into our room.

I forget about the creepy woman for the next several hours while Aftermath ravishes my body like a starved man.

"Uh," I groan while stretching and roll onto my back. My body is sore in all the right places and I smile thinking about the way Aftermath made love to me all night long. My hand moves to his side of the bed and it's empty. Sitting up, I hear the shower on and make my way into the bathroom. Aftermath is in the shower and I finish up my business before joining him.

Riding Through Life   J. Lynn Lombard

I wrap my arms around his wide chest, nuzzling my face into his back. "Hmm..." Aftermath grumbles.

"Hmm... is right," I agree. My hands roam lower, gripping his hardening shaft in my small hand. I work my hand up and down several times making Aftermath groan.

"God, your hand feels good, but I know what would feel better." Aftermath gently removes my hand and turns around. He lifts me and my back hits cool tiles while Aftermath nuzzles my neck. He bites and nips at the skin, making my body quiver with need. With one smooth motion, he surges inside of me causing a low moan to escape my throat. Aftermath's hips piston up while he pushes me down onto him. In a few short thrusts, I reach my peak and quiver around him. Aftermath releases a low guttural groan as he swells and empties inside of me.

We're both breathing hard, coming back down from our blissful orgasm when Aftermath's alarm blares from his phone on the counter.

"Shit." Aftermath grumbles. "I forgot to tell you last night." He releases my body but doesn't give me an inch of room. His big frame surrounds me.

"Forgot to tell me what?" I question looking into his eyes.

"Torch, Playboy and I have to leave this morning for a job. It should hopefully only take us a few days to complete." I hold back a sigh of disappointment and Aftermath cups my chin. "You distracted me last night and I completely forgot."

Riding Through Life   J. Lynn Lombard

I raise an eyebrow, "I distracted you? If I remember right, you pinned me against the wall and the last thing we were doing was talking."

Aftermath smirks that sexy smirk that makes my knees weak. "You might be right about that. I'm so sorry I didn't tell you last night."

I settle my hands on Aftermath's shoulders, trying to soothe the regret on his face. "It's OK. I think the way we handled things last night was way better than me stressing about you being hurt while on a job."

Aftermath grins, "You're right." He turns off the water and grabs a towel. He dries off my body and wraps the towel around me before doing the same thing for him. He reaches for his phone and checks the time before putting it back down. "We have about an hour. I can think of other things we can do until I have to leave." He waggles his eyebrows and I burst out laughing.

His body encases mine and we spend the next hour together in peaceful bliss before we get dressed and head into the common room.

Riding Through Life   J. Lynn Lombard

Riding Through Life   J. Lynn Lombard

Chapter 9

Kensi

    Torch, Daisy and their twins are sitting together on the couch. Capone, Danyella, Blayze, Monica and Nina are sitting together across from Torch and Daisy. Nina is making faces at the twins, making them giggle. Red, Nadia holding Matthew, Derange, Jezebelle, Dagger and Trigger are at the bar. No one is drinking but they're all talking and relaxing. Tiny is talking to Syvannah and Exleigh with Pearl glaring at the trio. Pretty Boy is missing, probably with a patch bunny and Bones is talking to Aftermath's mom, Silver Grace, which causes Aftermath to growl low. I quirk an eyebrow at Aftermath's reaction but he doesn't say a word besides grumbles about how his mom is not a MILF and Bones better keep his bone in his pants around her.

    Seth and Knight are running back and forth, getting whatever any Club brother or their Ol' Lady needs. That's their duty as prospects. To prove their loyalty to the club and the brothers and Ol' Ladies. Aftermath and I take a chair next to Torch and Capone, me sitting on his lap. His hands roam all over my body, setting it on fire.

Riding Through Life   J. Lynn Lombard

Playboy saunters out of the hallway Aftermath and I just came from with the blonde from last night wrapped around him. She looks worse for wear in the light of day, but I won't judge who does what or when they do it. It's not my place. As long as her glaring looks don't wander in my direction, I'm fine with her being here.

Playboy leans down and whispers something in her ear. She giggles as her eyes shoot to Aftermath and me, biting her lip. I stiffen and Aftermath notices.

"What's wrong, Tiger?" he asks, moving a piece of hair from my face.

My chin lifts in Playboy's direction. Aftermath glances over there but doesn't say a word. "Does she think we'd be up for a foursome?" I ask perplexed at the way she is staring at us. "That woman is highly mistaken and if she doesn't get her nasty eyes off my man, I will remove them for her." I threaten.

Nadia hears my threat, glances over in Playboy's direction and rolls her eyes. "Don't worry about it, she's harmless. If anything, she needed a good dicking last night to snap her out of her funk."

Playboy walks the woman to the hallway that leads outside and she disappears out of sight. Once she's gone, I relax. "Something about her doesn't sit well with me." I ponder out loud. Aftermath stands up, scooping me with him.

"I have to get going." He says while sliding my body down his until my feet touch the floor. "Tiger, try to stay out of trouble while I'm gone and please leave

Riding Through Life					J. Lynn Lombard

that woman alone." Aftermath kisses the side of my neck, "The last thing I need to worry about is you ending up in jail for harassment before our wedding." His lips trail hot and wet up the column of my throat and I forget what we were talking about.

We walk hand in hand toward the garage. Torch, Daisy and the twins follow with Playboy behind them. The rest of the club is behind them. It's tradition that any time a member has to leave on business, the whole club sees them off, giving them a wish for safe passage. This is always the hardest part for me, but I pull up my panties and stay strong for Aftermath, even though I'm hurting on the inside.

Aftermath wraps his arms around my waist, pulling me against him. I lock my hands around his neck so our bodies are flush against each other. The top of my head comes to his chin but we fit perfectly together.

"I love you, Tiger," Aftermath says, burying his face in my neck. I can feel his chest heaving against mine and it almost breaks me.

"I love you too, Aftermath." I pull his face away from my neck and cup his cheeks in the palm of my hands. "Stay safe and I'll see you when you get back." Staring into Aftermath's eyes, they're red-rimmed but he doesn't shed a tear. He holds them back, which is good because if he started crying, I would too.

Aftermath's lips land on mine in a heated kiss that ends all too soon. I grab his helmet and Aftermath straddles his bike, slipping his helmet on his head. He

Riding Through Life   J. Lynn Lombard

fires his bike up, drowning out the emotions of everyone. I kiss him one last time and step back into Nadia's awaiting arms before I don't let him go. Aftermath winks at me then drops his bike in first before riding out of the garage with Torch and Playboy behind him.

"Come on, girl. I have just the thing to cheer you up." Nadia says pulling me back into the Clubhouse once the three men are out of sight. "Danyella and Monica are taking Matthew and the twins for a little while and the three of us are getting the fuck out of here. Grab your dancing shoes!"

The excitement in Nadia's voice pulls me out of the spiral of depression I was heading in and before I know it, the three of us are at her dance studio. Red, Trigger, Bones and Knight are outside the building guarding it. I think it's overkill, but it's pointless to argue.

Daisy and I follow Nadia to the back of the building where the dancers practice. She flips on some lights and the room is flooded in a soft glow. Nadia walks over to a radio set up in the corner and turns on some dance music.

"OK, ladies, this is your time to unwind and let the music move you." Nadia starts moving her body, shaking her hips like a belly dancer. She moves her arms up and down while rotating her body. Her long blonde hair is flowing freely down her back. She's beautiful when she moves.

Daisy closes her eyes and starts to move, letting the music take her away. Once the two of them are in their own beat, I follow suit. I'm not one to dance in

Riding Through Life   J. Lynn Lombard

front of others, but Nadia is my best friend and I've become close with Daisy, so I suck it up and let my stress and worries melt away. Gone is the stress about the wedding, gone is the stress about the Feds trying to get to my dad. I dance and dance until I'm covered in sweat and my legs can't move.

I collapse on the mat and try to catch my breath. "Wow, that was exhilarating!" I exclaim.

"I agree," Daisy responds plopping down beside me.

"This is why I love dancing," Nadia speaks while wiping the sweat from her chest with a towel. She tosses one to me and another to Daisy. "You forget about everything for a little while."

"Speaking of forgetting, are you going to tell me anything about the bitch who kept staring at my man like he was a piece of meat she wanted to sink her teeth into?" I blurt out. I have no filter when it comes to certain things. Which can be good but it can be bad too.

"I can answer that for you." I turn around and find the bitch of the hour standing in the doorway.

I stand up and cross my arms over my chest. "Well?" I prompt, not the least bit worried about her hearing me call her a bitch.

"Your honesty is refreshing, Kensi." She states. "Must be hard to be so honest when others you trust can withhold the truth from you and not bat an eye."

Riding Through Life   J. Lynn Lombard

Her breathy voice is getting on my nerves and I'm close to knocking her on her ass.

"What the hell are you talking about?" Questions swirling around in my brain. Who is lying to me? Is it someone I trust? What is she talking about? Does someone know about the visit to my dad's house? Is the FBI harassing my family?

"Don't ask me the question, ask someone you trust with your whole heart." With those parting words, she turns around and disappears out of sight.

Anger replaces confusion and I take off after this bitch. "Kensi, where are you going?" Nadia shouts from across the room.

I don't slow down when I answer back, over my shoulder. "She is *not* coming in here and accusing people like that!" I hurry out of the dance studio and sprint down the hallway. I stop at the reception desk, turning my head left and right. I listen for footsteps, but all I can hear is my harsh breathing. Deciding to check outside, I burst through the glass doors.

Bones jumps a mile high, clutching his chest. "Fuck, Kensi. You gave me a heart attack."

"Where'd she go?" I ask, look around the parking lot. It's empty aside from the SUV we brought and Knight's and Bones' bikes.

"Where'd who go?" Bones asks, still rubbing his chest.

Riding Through Life   J. Lynn Lombard

"Uh! Never mind." I throw my hands up and go back inside. Nadia and Daisy are still in the dancing room and hurry over to me.

"What was that all about?" Daisy questions.

"I have no idea, but we're going to find out," I answer, pulling both women into the security room with me. If the bitch wants to fucking play, I'll play.

Red is in here at the monitors. He looks up when we barge in, pushing his glasses up. "What the fuck?"

"I need you to pull up the feed from a few minutes ago," I demand.

"What? Why?" Red questions.

"Because the bitch wants to play games and fuck with my head. When I get my hands on her, I'll fuck with her head," I respond.

"Who is she talking about?" Red asks, peering behind me at Nadia.

"Lynn, my new dance instructor. She came in here all cryptic about people Kensi trusts," Nadia answers.

Red's eyes narrow and he swallows hard before standing up. "Sorry, I can't help." Red ushers us out of the security room and shuts the door behind us, locking it.

"What's going on? Why aren't you helping me?" I ask. I'd stomp my foot if it didn't make me look like a child throwing a temper tantrum.

Riding Through Life   J. Lynn Lombard

"Nothing is going on. If you ladies are done dancing, we have to get back to the Clubhouse." Red's face flushes, but his gaze never wavers. "I can see you have questions, Kensi. But think about everything before you fly off the handle."

I know he is hiding something from me and I will find out. I take Red's advice while we drive back to the Clubhouse. Aftermath's been very attentive the last few weeks, more than normal. I'll catch him spacing out every once in a while like he's thinking about something that he shouldn't be thinking about. He doesn't want to socialize when there's a party. No scratch that. He'll socialize with Club members and their Ol' Ladies, but he won't socialize when a certain blonde comes strutting in.

My heart sinks with realization as Red pulls into the Clubhouse driveway. I don't say a word to anyone as I drag my feet into our room. My stomach is flipping violently and I feel like I'm going to be sick. If Aftermath is cheating on me with that skank, they're both going to regret it. I'm not a doormat, nor will I ever be a doormat.

The smell of him lingers in our room and it makes my eyes tear up. I can't stay here. If I do, I'll break and allow Aftermath to walk all over me with his lies. I've had enough people lying to me in my life, I don't need him to do it too.

Quickly, I pack all the stuff I can into a couple of suitcases and stop at the foot of the bed. It's still messy from earlier today when we made love before he left. I can't stop the tears as they slide down my face anymore. Taking a deep breath, I slip the engagement ring off my finger and set it on the dresser. I can't do this.

Riding Through Life   J. Lynn Lombard

    Some people might think I'm rushing to judge, but those people don't know the hell I went through to get to where I am today. I refuse to allow a liar and a cheater into my life. Even if he didn't sleep with that dancer, something happened and until Aftermath tells me the truth, I can't stay here.

Riding Through Life   J. Lynn Lombard

Chapter 10

Aftermath

"Have you located her yet?" I ask Red. I called him the moment his text came through about Kensi missing. No one has seen her for a few days and I haven't had cell phone service out here in BFE until now.

"Her SUV is at her dad's house but she isn't answering," Red responds. "I don't know what is going on."

"I don't know either and I'm stuck here for another few days. I'll try calling her. If she doesn't answer, will you send Nadia over to check on her?" I don't understand why Kensi would leave without a word to anyone. Is she in trouble? Is she being forced to leave?

"Yeah, brother, I will. Let me know if you hear anything." Red answers.

"Thanks, brother. Keep in touch." I hang up the phone before Red can respond.

We've been stuck out here in the middle of nowhere BFE and our cell phones don't work unless

Riding Through Life   J. Lynn Lombard

we're back at the seedy motel we're staying in. Which is the only motel in a thirty mile radius from where we believe the young girl is being held.

"Everything OK?" Torch asks, looking up from his phone. He isn't carefree and happy like he normally is. This trip is taking a toll on both of us.

"I don't know. Kensi left sometime a few days ago and no one can reach her." Playboy snorts from his bed across the room and my eyes narrow. "You got something to say?"

"Nah, man. Go call your woman." Playboy responds, closing his eyes. "That's what I'd do if I were you."

Playboy's attitude has been shitty this whole trip, making it impossible to rest when we need to. "I don't know what your fucking issue is, but if you have something to say, by all means say it," I growl.

"I don't have shit to say to you. You disgust me." Playboy stands up and collects his things from his dresser. "Fuck this, I'm out." He slips on his boots and stomps out the door, slamming it behind him.

"What the hell was that about?" I ask.

"I have no clue. The boy has been a ticking time bomb since the head injury he received when protecting Jezebelle and Seth. I think the assholes hit him too hard or something." Torch responds.

"That or they didn't hit him hard enough." I snort. "I'm going to try and reach Kensi. Something is up and I need to figure out what."

Riding Through Life   J. Lynn Lombard

"Go for it. I'll be here missing my kids and Ol' Lady." Torch sighs lying down on his bed and closing his eyes. This shit is hitting Torch pretty hard but we gotta do what we gotta do for the sake of the club. And it should only be a couple more days, then we can get home.

Closing the door behind me, I step onto the cracked concrete and wander further away from our room. The wind slightly picks up and a tumbleweed spins past me, lost in its path. I wander to the back of the motel for privacy and better cell phone service. The desert sweeps on for miles. The sun is starting to set, painting the sky in deep reds and purples. I lean against the concrete building and dial Kensi's number. It rings several times before going to voicemail. My heart plummets into my toes. This isn't right. Kensi never sends me to voicemail.

I try calling her three more times with the same results. Not to be the one to give up, I try again and her sweet voice picks up on the fourth ring.

"What?" Just one word portrays the anguish and heartbreak in Kensi's tone.

"Tiger, what's going on?" I ask, clearing a lump in my throat.

"I don't want to get into this right now, Aftermath," Kensi whispers.

"Get into what? Kensi, what is going on? C'mon, baby, I can't fix this if I don't have a clue what has you running." I plead.

Riding Through Life   J. Lynn Lombard

A long pause settles between us and Kensi snorts, "I'm not running, Aftermath. I'm done." Her voice is stronger now, anger clear in her tone. "Until you can come clean and be honest with me, I'm fucking done."

Kensi hangs up the phone before I can respond, leaving my head reeling with questions. I call back, but it goes right to voicemail. "Fuck!" I grip my phone in my hand, surprised it doesn't crush under the strain.

Dialing Red, I grind my teeth. He picks up on the second ring. "Yo, did you get ahold of her?"

"What the fuck happened?" I ask with anger lacing my tone.

"What the fuck do you mean? Nothing happened." Red growls back. "Look, I know this is frustrating, brother, but you need to focus on getting this job done and then worry about what's going on with Kensi. I'll send Seth and Knight over with Nadia to check on her but that's the best I can do right now. I know it sucks, but the Club comes first." Red hangs up the phone and I punch the concrete wall I'm leaning against. My knuckles bloom with blood.

"Fuck!" I scream into the twilight. I let Kensi's words run through my head. *Until you can come clean and be honest with me, I'm fucking done. Come clean. Be honest with me. I'm done.* "Shit."

Storming back into our hotel room, I fling open the door, letting it hit the wall. Torch is still lying on his bed, staring at his phone. Either Daisy sent him naked pictures or twin pictures. From the sad look on his face,

Riding Through Life   J. Lynn Lombard

I'd say the latter and he's missing his kids. Playboy is also lying on his bed, his phone in his hand. He glares at me and rolls away.

"C'mon boys, get the fuck up. I'm done playing cat and mouse with these fuckers. We're going in tonight and going home." I stomp my way over to my side of the room and start throwing shit in my bag.

"What the hell are you rambling about?" Torch stands up and starts packing his shit too. Playboy hasn't moved yet.

"Like you give a shit about going home." Playboy grumbles.

Ignoring him and his pissy ass mood for the last couple of days, I answer Torch. "I'm talking about going in and getting the girl then getting the fuck out, tonight. I don't know why we're sitting around here with our thumbs up our asses. We know where she is, and how many guards she has. We're going in, fucking shit up and then going home to our women."

"It's about damn time. Being here with you isn't my idea of a fun time." Playboy throws his phone on his bed and a picture of the woman who came onto me catches my attention.

I pick up his phone before he can grab it. "What the fuck is this?" I demand.

"Not your fucking business." Playboy tries to grab his phone out of my hand but I don't let him. "Give me my fucking phone." He tries to swipe his phone again, but I put him on his ass with one hit to his jaw.

I scroll through the messages and anger surges through my veins. "You know this is a lie." I rant. The more I read, the more pissed off I become. "This bitch is a liar."

"Says you," Playboy stands up, wiping the blood off his lip and snatches his phone back. "Tell me you didn't see her naked." I don't answer because it would be pointless to lie. "Tell me you didn't *bump* into her at the grocery store with Pearl and Lexi." He air quotes the word bump.

"How the fuck do you know?" I ask.

"She told me the night I fucked her at the Clubhouse."

"What did she say?"

"She said she was wrong to fuck one brother and then another, especially when she said she didn't know the first brother was unavailable."

"Why would you assume it was me?"

"I didn't. She's the one who told me who it was. Lynn said she felt guilty the next morning because the one with the multi-colored eyes had no idea what kind of asshole her man is. Kensi is the only one with those eyes." Playboy responds.

"Is this why Kensi left and you've been a dick this whole time?" I ask, not expecting a response but Playboy gives it to me anyway.

Riding Through Life   J. Lynn Lombard

"I'd fucking leave your ass too if you were cheating on me, asshole." Playboy seethes.

"What? You cheated on Kensi? When? Where? How the fuck?" Torch pipes in.

"I didn't cheat on Kensi!" I shout.

"Then explain to me what the fuck is going on." Torch demands, crossing his arms over his massive chest. As the enforcer of the Royal Bastards, you have to be one big motherfucker and Torch is just that. His shaved head and tattoos make him a scary son-of-a-bitch and one person ahead of me as our Sgt at arms.

I exhale a deep breath and sit down on my bed, running out of steam. "I didn't touch that psycho bitch. When Red and I were at Nadia's dance studio a couple of weeks ago, he was updating their security and I was getting restless. So, I went to make sure all the doors were locked and no one was there. The woman's locker room was unlocked so I went inside. After calling out several times and no one answered, I went in. I cleared the showers and stalls and on the way out, I had to sit down. I was a ball of nerves going in there and I don't know why. That's when it happened." I hang my head. "That chick came out of nowhere, naked as the day she came through her mama's cunt. She tried to come on to me and I yanked her hand off my arm and got the fuck out of there. I didn't see her again until she ran into me and the girls at the store. She ran into me, I wasn't looking for her and the innuendos she was throwing, Pearl and Lexi were catching. She insinuated we slept together when we didn't. Then having her show up at the Clubhouse our last night at home, threw me for a loop. I don't know what this bitch is playing at, but I never touched her and I don't want to. It wasn't my choice to see her naked and I didn't ask for her to come onto me." That's it. That's the whole story and I feel better getting it off my chest, like a weight has been lifted.

Torch is scowling, making him more menacing. "Why didn't you tell Kensi?"

I pick my head up and glare at Torch. "What?"

"Why didn't you tell Kensi about this?"

"Why would I? Nothing happened."

"Because, dumbass," Playboy pipes in. "If you would have told her the truth, none of this would have happened and that bitch wouldn't have been allowed in the Clubhouse and she would have been fired from Nadia's dance studio."

"Fuck." I scrub my hands down my face when the realization hits. "Because I didn't do anything, she spun it to make me the bad guy. Who is this crazy bitch?"

"That's what we're going to find out." Torch pulls his phone from his pocket and dials Red. "Hey did you run a background on Nadia's new dancer, Lynn?" The line is silent for a beat while Red replies. "Well, something isn't adding up, not if this bitch can come between brothers and their Ol' ladies." Torch motions for Playboy to give him his phone. "Run this number and see what you can come up with. Then when you're done, check Playboy's room for any of her fingerprints.

Riding Through Life   J. Lynn Lombard

She isn't being honest with us." Torch rattles off the number to Red. "And keep this between the four of us. I don't want anyone else, not even Nadia to know about this until we have all the details. I'll run it by Capone when we get home. Thanks, brother." Torch hangs up his phone and shoves it in his pocket. "Let's get our mark and fuck shit up so we can get back home."

Riding Through Life   J. Lynn Lombard

Riding Through Life   J. Lynn Lombard

Chapter 11

Kensi

A weight is sitting on my chest and all I can do at the moment is cry. Aftermath was everything to me. He was the man I wanted to spend the rest of my life with. Now all my dreams are shattered lying in a million pieces at my feet. Every time I move, I'm cut with the realization that Aftermath didn't love me, not if he could do what he did.

Somehow that bitch got my number and has been texting me shit about Aftermath no one but me should know. She told me how they met and she feels guilty for letting it carry on the way it did, not knowing she was the other woman.

At first, I didn't believe her, but after a while, it started to make sense. The way Aftermath would do things for me out of guilt of hiding something or the way he'd space out like he was thinking about something, or I should say someone that wasn't me. And each time she saw him, we weren't together.

Then there's the Club. According to Lynn, at the party, Aftermath and she were going to announce their

Riding Through Life   J. Lynn Lombard

new relationship and move me out. But apparently, that didn't go as planned. She told me it was because I swept in and stole him away before they could. That hurt my heart and shattered my soul. When I asked her if that was the case, why did she sleep with Playboy? She told me it was because she wanted to make Aftermath jealous with envy. Something isn't sitting right with her story.

A sob escapes from my chest when my phone rings with Aftermath's ringtone. It's been a few days since I left the Clubhouse and not a single person had reached out to me. I must be as disposable as those Club Bunnies. Now that Aftermath and I aren't together, I don't belong there and they've all proved it with their actions. I stare at my phone, contemplating whether to answer or not when it quits ringing and goes to voicemail. It immediately starts ringing again and I can't escape the tears running down my face. Why did he have to do this?

It stops and starts again two more times. Aftermath isn't going to let this go until I answer him. Might as well start now.

"What?" My voice is trembling with heartbreak.

"Tiger, what's going on?" Aftermath's voice is a soothing balm to my broken heart.

"I don't want to get into this right now, Aftermath," I whisper, holding back tears.

"Get into what? Kensi, what is going on?" The confusion and pain in his voice is my undoing. I sob

Riding Through Life   J. Lynn Lombard

quietly, letting my tears fall. "C'mon, baby, I can't fix this if I don't have a clue what has you running."

I pause for a long time, anger replacing sadness. He's confused and wants to fix this? Maybe if he'd kept his dick in his pants this wouldn't have happened. "I'm not running, Aftermath. I'm done." My voice is stronger now, anger clear in my tone. "Until you can come clean and be honest with me, I'm fucking done." I hang up the phone and throw it across the room.

I'm at my dad's new house, in the spare room. When I showed up on his doorstep, he didn't hesitate to take me into his arms and try to soothe my broken heart the best way he could. We got drunk the first night, passing the bottle of Tequila back and forth until neither of us could talk anymore. The second night, after nursing my hangover and swearing off Tequila and men, he made me my favorite comfort food, grilled cheese and tomato soup. That night I cried myself to sleep. Tonight, he left me alone and is giving me space.

It's been several hours since I last talked to Aftermath. My eyes are red and gritty from crying, my throat hurts and my chest is heavy. The rumble of motorcycles in the distance has my heart hammering in my chest. There is no way Aftermath is back already. I stand up and pull the curtain back slightly, looking down onto the street from the second-floor window. A single black SUV is still parked outside but if someone is in it, they haven't moved in the past six hours. The rumble of Harleys grows louder until they quiet down and

Riding Through Life   J. Lynn Lombard

disappear. When I don't see anyone turning into the driveway, I push back the curtain and flop onto the bed.

This is supposed to be a happy time in my life, not one of the worst. I'm fucking over being sad. Anger replaces the hurt I'm suffering from, and I pull myself off the bed. Heading into the attached bathroom, I turn on the shower as hot as I can stand it.

Peeling off my stinky clothes, I get in the shower and let the hot water soothe my aching muscles and painful heart. Once the hot water turns cold, I get out and dry myself off. I clean off the steam from the mirror over the sink and stare at myself. I'm a beautiful young woman with everything going for me. If a man cannot appreciate what I have to offer, then he doesn't deserve my heart or my soul. I just wish none of this was true and the heartbreak didn't happen.

I need answers, damn it and the only way I'll get them is from Aftermath. Not over the phone or through text messages. Face to face. If he did cheat on me, then I'll walk away with a bruised heart but my head held high. If he didn't, he has a lot of explaining why he wasn't honest with me about this chick.

With renewed determination, I throw on a pair of jeans and a tight white T-shirt. I fix my hair and makeup and exit my bathroom. If Aftermath wants this skank, there isn't anything I can do but make him regret ever giving her the time of day. If it's all a lie, I'll be wearing my ass-kickers and beat some skanky ass.

Hurrying down the stairs, I hear my dad moving around in the kitchen, "Hey Dad! I'm going to head out for a little while!"

Riding Through Life   J. Lynn Lombard

"Kensi..." The calmness I felt earlier disappears when I hear my dad's voice. It isn't fear but the authoritative tone he used to use when something wasn't right and he wanted me to comply without question.

I stop in my tracks when the front door busts open and six men in suits come barging in with their guns drawn. "What the fuck!" I shout as they surround me.

Not to be taken down lightly and compliantly, I go after the bigger guy. My fist connects with his face before he knows what's happening. Pain vibrates up my arm and into my shoulder but I don't let it stop me. I fight, kick, scream, scratch and bite, giving them everything I have. One after another try holding me down, but I keep fighting.

"Enough!" Someone bellows before smacking me upside the head with something hard, making me dizzy. The knock stuns me enough that the six men can subdue me.

Once they have me secure with zip ties around my wrists, behind my back and my feet tied together, do they bring in my dad by gunpoint. The man who knocked me upside the head keeps his gun trained on my dad's head. My heart is hammering inside my chest, and questions are swirling in my brain. Something wet and sticky slithers down the left side of my face below the spot where this asshole hit me.

Riding Through Life   J. Lynn Lombard

When my dad sees me tied up and bleeding, he loses it. Their mistake is not tying him up the way they did me. He fights them with everything he has and everything he was trained to do. Even though my hands are secure behind my back and my feet are tied together, I still do what I can to help my dad. I trip, kick and knee anyone who gets in my path.

Suddenly my head is yanked back and my hair is on fire from the roots. I scream in pain as I feel something cold pressed to the side of my head. "Stop! Or I'll kill this bitch." The click of the safety on a gun vibrates in my ear and I stop fighting.

My dad stops as well with his hands up in the air. "You don't want to do this."

"Oh, I think I do. For some reason, my superior wants you back with them and I was told by all means necessary to make it happen. This is my necessity." He pushes the gun harder against the side of my head and I whimper. "Now, get on the ground on your stomach with your hands above your head. If you move, I will shoot her in the face." The man snarls.

Watching helplessly while my dad complies with this request sends a tear down my cheek. He's tough and brave, but when it comes to his little girl, he will do anything he can to keep me safe. Once my dad's hands are secure behind his back and his feet tied, they move us. It's slow going since neither of us can walk normally. This freaking sucks big time.

"Kensi," my dad whispers once we're in the back of the SUV that was parked across the street.

Riding Through Life   J. Lynn Lombard

"Dad?" I whisper back. My head is killing me but I keep my wits about me.

"I'm so sorry this happened, Lil' Kay." The pain in his voice is breaking my heart.

"It's not your fault, Dad. We didn't know they'd go to this extreme to get you to come back." I yawn, my head pounding against my skull. "I'm so tired."

"Lil' Kay, stay awake. Don't fall asleep on me." Dad nudges me with his shoulder.

My eyes drift shut and I snap them back open. "I'm trying."

"Try harder. If you have a concussion and fall asleep, you might not wake back up." The pleading in my dad's voice snaps me out of my exhaustion.

I yawn again. "My whole body hurts, Dad. If I sleep for a little while, I'll be good to go." I close my eyes and darkness takes hold of me.

Riding Through Life   J. Lynn Lombard

Chapter 12

Kensi

The fog is lifted from my brain and I dream about Aftermath finding me and telling me this was all a dream. Everything that happened wasn't real. He didn't cheat on me with that skank. That everything was a lie to break us apart and he loves me with everything he has.

"Kensi?" I feel Aftermath's hands on my body, shaking me. Why is he shaking me?

"Kensi?" He shakes harder. "C'mon, Lil' Kay, wake up." Why does Aftermath sound like my Dad?

"No, Mark, I don't want to leave." I groan through the pain in my head. I blink my eyes open and immediately snap them shut when the bright light hits them. "Ouch." I move my hands to rub the side of my head but they won't move.

"What the fuck?"

"Hang on, Lil' Kay. Keep your eyes closed for a second." Something heavy is set over my face. "Try opening your eyes now." My dad instructs.

Riding Through Life   J. Lynn Lombard

I blink a few times and the light isn't as harsh. I have a towel over my eyes. "Can't you turn the lights off?"

"No, I can't." I try to sit up but the room spins around me. "Easy, Kensi." My dad's strong hands wrap around my shoulders, helping me sit up, keeping the blanket or whatever it is over my head.

"Why are my hands tied?" I question, wiggling my numb fingers.

"Because I couldn't undo them with you unconscious. Do you remember how I taught you to get out of zip ties?" I nod my head even though it hurts. "I'm going to need you to do that now, Lil' Kay. Once you get free, then we can get out of here."

"Where is here?" I ask while painstakingly moving my arms from behind my back, under my butt to in front of me. "Can I take this thing off my head so I can see?"

"How does your head feel?"

"Like a million gnomes are playing basketball on a concrete slab and jackhammering at the same time." I groan.

"Then, no. Leave the towel on until we get out of here." I feel my dad's arm rest on my shoulder. "Now, I need you to snap your zip ties for me."

I inhale a deep breath moving my wrists up and yanking them down and apart in a fast motion. Pain shoots through my wrists up my arms but the zip ties give way and my hands are free. "Shit. That hurt."

Riding Through Life   J. Lynn Lombard

"Good job, Lil' Kay. Now you need to do that with your feet." My dad praises me.

I take a deep breath and repeat the movements I did with my arms and wrists with my legs and feet. It takes a couple of times, but I finally get the zip ties to break apart. My head is pounding even harder and I feel like I'm going to throw up.

"Let me help you up and then we can get out of here." Dad carefully helps me stand and a wave of dizziness takes hold. Bile climbs its way up my throat and I lean over and vomit. "It's OK, Kensi, let it out and then we can get moving."

"Where are we and what happened to those monkey suits?" I ask between dry heaves. Once I feel my stomach is empty and I'm not going to vomit, I slowly stand up. "Fuck, my head hurts."

"They dropped us off in this apartment complex and left one guy to guard us. The assholes misjudged me and my capabilities." I can hear the smirk in my dad's voice. "He's currently nursing a bad headache with a few cracked ribs while he's hogtied and gagged."

"Did they say what they wanted? Why they did this to us?" We slowly move and since I can't see where I'm going, my dad has ahold of my arm guiding me.

"The one dick said he was from the FBI, but I don't believe it. It smells like a cover-up for a case I've been working on."

Riding Through Life   J. Lynn Lombard

"What makes you think that?" I have to stop for a moment and catch my breath. Who knew being hit on the head would make you breathless?

"Because the FBI doesn't kidnap and beat people who don't want to join them. And it's a feeling I got. They don't smell like Feds to me. Remember, I used to be one?"

I snort, making my head pound. "Ouch." I rub my temple and wince.

"I'll take a look at it once we get out of these bright lights."

"Why can't you turn them off?" I ask again.

"It would alert the others that something is wrong and they'll come back. And we're not walking out the front door, we're going down the fire escape. That is the only place where there isn't a camera. Come on, we're almost there." Dad carefully leads me down a hallway and into a room.

A cold breeze blows across my body and despite the warm clothes I have on, I shiver. My teeth chatter causing my head to hurt. "Damn, this sucks."

"We'll be out of here in no time and get you checked out," Dad assures me. "Ok, are you ready?"

"Can I take this towel off my head?"

"Once we step outside you can. But don't look down. If you have a concussion, it will make the vertigo worse." Dad takes my hand and guides me out of the window. "Ok, slowly remove the towel and blink but be prepared, even this light might be too much."

I remove the towel and close my eyes, preparing myself for the harsh lights invading my eyeballs. When I open my eyes, I'm greeted with darkness and only a street lamp glowing dimly in the night. "This I can handle."

"Good, Lil' Kay. Let's get the hell out of here." Dad responds. "I'll go first and you follow. That way if you slip, I can catch you."

Taking a deep breath, I nod my head, "Let's do this."

We slowly make our way down the rickety old fire escape, having to stop a few times when dizziness takes hold of me. Luckily, I don't throw up again, even though I want to. Once we reach the bottom, Dad and I search around for a car or something we can borrow to get the hell out of here. Not finding anything, we take off on foot.

"Where are we going?" I ask after an hour of walking. We're in the middle of nowhere and it's so dark, I have no clue where we are.

"We're almost there, Lil' Kay. Just a few more miles and we'll be to safety." Dad answers cryptically. I follow along, trusting him to keep us safe and protected. My mind keeps replaying back to the beginning of this whole shitshow. Wishing I made different choices when it came to the decision to leave Aftermath.

Riding Through Life   J. Lynn Lombard

After drowning in my doubts and making my head hurt worse, I bite the bullet and ask my dad the question I should have asked when this all started. "Dad, do you think I overreacted in this whole situation with Aftermath?"

Dad stops walking and turns to look me over. "I think you're miserable and in pain, Lil' Kay. Your trust has been broken along with your heart. I don't think you overreacted, but I do think you weren't being rational."

"He called me earlier tonight and I hung up the phone on him. Should I have let him explain?"

He releases a deep breath, "I think the two of you love each other enough to get past whatever happened. What is it exactly you're afraid of?"

What am I afraid of? I think about this question long and hard before answering. "I'm afraid of being like Mom and leaving when things get tough," I whisper. "Crap. I did exactly what she did to you, didn't I?"

Dad offers me a tight smile. "There's a difference between you and your mom, Lil' Kay. You're worried you're like her, but you're not. I know this because you have regretted leaving the way you did and she didn't." Dad wraps me in a warm hug. "No matter what, you will always have my support, but I do think you need to hear Aftermath out and figure out where to go from there."

"Thanks, Dad. And by the way, Mom's an idiot for treating you the way she did. You're kind of badass." I genuinely smile for the first time in a few days.

"I am pretty awesome. Which I learned from my headstrong daughter." He kisses the side of my head that isn't bleeding and we continue to walk.

After another two hours and several stops later, bright lights come into view, making me wince. After blinking away tears, my eyes adjust to where we are. The Royal Bastards MC Clubhouse comes into view. This is the last place I want to be right now even knowing I need to talk to Aftermath.

"Shit."

Riding Through Life					J. Lynn Lombard

Riding Through Life   J. Lynn Lombard

Chapter 13

Aftermath

"Let's do this shit." Torch exclaims raising his mask to cover his face. Torch, Playboy and I are in black tactical gear, ready to take down these low-life motherfuckers. I watch Torch's eyes light up when he hits a button on his phone. A loud explosion permeates the air a few beats later, shaking the ground under our feet. Men come running out of the house, investigating the explosion. Several of their vehicles are on fire and it's spreading fast. They try to put the fire out and we sneak around them in the shadows.

"Big Bang, motherfuckers." Torch's excited voice echoes through the darkness.

"Come on," I order, moving through the shadows toward a rundown ranch-style home. Why do these assholes always have to use a rundown shack or house in the middle of nowhere or an abandoned warehouse or hotel? Don't they have any class? Yeah, you're an asshole for kidnapping and abusing women, but at least have some dignity.

Riding Through Life   J. Lynn Lombard

My mind drifts back to finding Kensi in that rundown warehouse basement with Danyella years ago chained to a bed, raped and beaten, without hope. God, I'm such a fuck up. She has been through so much in her young life, everything she has been through and came out of, the security she placed in my hands has been ripped away by my foolishness. The trust she had in me was shattered because I didn't tell her about that skank coming on to me and letting Kensi believe the lies spewed about her and me.

Red called me before we left and told me he hacked into this bitch's phone. Her name is Lynn Martinez and she's from Oklahoma, moving here two months ago. He also said something didn't add up on her timeline so he was digging further into it. She had been texting Kensi, telling her all kinds of lies about us. Instead of calling Kensi to set the record straight, I put it on the back burner until this is over.

"Aftermath, get your fucking head in the game, brother. You can fix Kensi later, but you can't do that if you're dead." Torch growls in frustration.

"I'm with you, Torch. Let's go." We find an unlocked window in the back of the house and crawl inside. One by one, the three of us snap the necks of the guards creeping around the house as we come to them. We don't use our guns because that will draw attention to us where we don't need it.

Clearing each room, we finally find our mark. She's naked and handcuffed to the frame of the bed, bruised and beaten. Blood is trickling down the side of her head and between her thighs that are covered with

Riding Through Life   J. Lynn Lombard

fresh bruises. Rage like no other penetrates my soul when I look at this teenager and Kensi's face comes into view instead. I roar in frustration and leave the room. I kick and stomp the first dead body I find until his face is unrecognizable. Then I move to the next and the next.

One of the men who was outside with the fire comes barging into the house and when he spots me, he raises his gun and fires off a shot. It barely misses my ear and I'm on him like white on rice. I start punching him in the face repeatedly until he stops breathing. Then I punch him some more. All while thinking about the abuse Kensi suffered in that basement. Then I stomp on his body, thinking about my fuck up with Kensi and how I didn't protect her from me.

Strong arms pull me off the dead guy and turn me to face them. I'm ready to pound someone else until Torch's voice invades my headspace. "ENOUGH!"

I blink and the room comes into focus. Playboy is cradling the young girl wrapped in a blanket in his arms. Her head is resting on his chest. "I'm good. I'm good." I respond holding my bloody knuckles up.

I spit on the dead guy and walk out the back door, making sure no one has the jump on us. Once the coast is clear, the three of us walk rapidly to the SUV we brought from the hotel, instead of our bikes. Once Playboy is settling in the back with the girl, I jump in the driver's seat and Torch gets in the passenger seat. He pulls out his phone and clicks another button. A fireball explodes behind us, making the mirrors light up like the Fourth of July.

Riding Through Life   J. Lynn Lombard

"Boom, dead motherfuckers." Torch declares. The whole area is on fire and explosion after explosion rocks the ground and shakes our SUV. No one will be able to escape that hell.

Once we get a safe distance away, Torch calls Capone putting it on speakerphone.

Capone answers in the first ring. "Tell me good news."

"Package is secure and the office is blown away by the speed of our services." He's always saying weird shit like this and it drives everyone nuts, but that's who Torch is. Take it or fuck off is what he says.

"We've got another issue, am I on speakerphone?" Capone asks. The tension in his voice makes me sit up straight in the driver's seat.

"Aye, Prez. All three of us can hear you." Torch responds.

"Good, now listen. Aftermath, I don't want you to go off the rails but something's happened." My heart hammers against my chest and my stomach sinks to my toes. "Nadia, Knight and Seth went to Kensi's Dad's house." Capone pauses.

My breathing is erratic and every bad situation comes flooding into my mind. Kensi is gone, she's hurt, she's bleeding out and no one can fix her, she's dead, or her dad is dead. "What is it, Prez?" I growl trying to keep my temper in check.

Capone releases a deep sigh. "The house was broken into and both Sheriff Donovan and Kensi are missing. Red has been looking for them with no luck. From the images we have, they were thrown into the back of a dark SUV. Kensi wasn't moving on her own and Sheriff Donovan was tied with a gun pointed at his head. That's all the information we have."

"Son of a bitch!" I shout, smacking the steering wheel. "God damn it!"

"Aftermath, calm the fuck down." Capone demands through the phone. "We have our best guys on this and as soon as they hear anything, I will let you know."

"What about the girl?" Playboy asks from the backseat. He is still cradling the teenager we rescued. "If our contact is missing, what do we do with her? We were supposed to take her to him."

"Good point," Capone commends. "Bring her here and the girls will keep her safe and comfortable. I'll arrange a room for her and Derange and Jezebelle will look her over." Capone pauses. "Look, I know this isn't ideal, but Aftermath, there is nothing you can do right now anyway. What I need you to do is get all four of you back here safely and then we will assess the situation again. Hopefully, by the time you get here, Red will have some answers." The line goes dead and I scream in frustration.

I should be there looking for my woman, no one else. If I wasn't such an ass, Kensi wouldn't be in this situation. I can't help but shoulder all of the blame.

Riding Through Life   J. Lynn Lombard

"We'll figure it out, brother," Torch rests a comforting hand on my shoulder. "And when we do, you will beg Kensi for forgiveness and together you'll handle this shit."

I pray to the Biker Gods that Torch is right. I pray things won't be so irreparable that we don't stand a chance. For the first time in my life, I pray to a God I never believed in that Kensi comes back to me unharmed.

Riding Through Life   J. Lynn Lombard

Chapter 14

Aftermath

    We pull into the Clubhouse around midnight and Derange is waiting for us at the door. He hurries over to the SUV with Jezebelle right behind him. He yanks the back passenger side door open before I even have a chance to put it in Park. "How's she doing? Did she wake up? Is she in pain?" Doctor Derange fires off questions while putting a stethoscope on the young girl's chest and listening to her lungs. That's what Capone's daughter Nina started calling him a few months ago when she decided to become adventurous and jumped off some beams in the house they're building. I could have sworn Capone's heart stopped when he heard her scream in pain. She sprained her ankle and wrist, but it could have been much worse if she was higher up. Nina hasn't done that again, but I imagine over time she will do something like that again. Every time someone is hurt, it's Derange and Jezebelle that mend them back together.

    "She hasn't woken up since before we got to her. Her breathing is there but shallow and I think whatever drug they gave her, it's kept her sedated."

Riding Through Life   J. Lynn Lombard

Playboy holds up the girl's arm and shows Derange the track marks. "She also has fresh bruising and blood on the inside of her thighs." He tucks her arm back inside the blanket to keep her warm.

"Bring her inside and we'll take it from here. Thank you, Playboy, for keeping her comfortable." Playboy climbs out of the car and Derange shuts the door. Jezebelle opens the door that leads into the Clubhouse and they disappear out of sight.

I release the breath I didn't realize I was holding and squeeze my eyes shut. When I open them, Torch is still in the vehicle with me and he squeezes my shoulder. "We'll find her, Aftermath. Have faith." Torch climbs out of the SUV and shuts the door behind him. Once he's out of sight, I get out, shut the door and rest my body against it. Pulling my phone out, I dial Kensi's number. I know she won't answer but I have to try something. It rings several times before it goes to voicemail so I leave her a message.

"Tiger, I'm sorry things went the way they did. If I had realized how much of a domino effect this decision made, I would have told you about that chick coming on to me. I didn't think it was a big deal at the time, but now I see that it was. I'm so sorry for not being upfront and honest. I know I shattered your trust in me, but I'm willing to do whatever it takes to make it up to you. I love you, Kensi. You own my mind, body, heart and soul. It only beats for you and will until my dying breath. Come back to me, please. I'm not whole without you." I hang up the phone and push back the tears threatening to tumble down my cheeks. Instead, I squeeze my hands into tight fists, the dried blood cracking.

Riding Through Life   J. Lynn Lombard

Commotion from the guard shack gathers my attention. Knight and Seth are assigned guard duty when they don't have something to do for the Club. I hear shouting but I'm too far away to make out voices. Capone and Red come flying out of the Clubhouse with Blayze, Trigger and Torch hot on their heels.

"What the fuck is going on?" I ask. No one answers so I follow behind them. Being the SSA, it's my duty to protect the club and its members. I've been doing a shitty job these last few days. "STOP!" I shout, causing everyone who was moving to slow down. I know I can get my rank pulled but damn it, my Prez needs to let me protect him. "Prez, let me take the lead and do my fucking job. I'm supposed to protect you, not sit back and watch someone shoot your ass and if you want to reprimand me later, I'll welcome your punishment. Torch and Trigger, you're with me. Blayze and Capone, stay behind us until we can assess the situation."

Capone's nostrils flare, but he knows I'm right. He steps back with Blayze and they fall in behind us. "Knight, what's going on up there?" I shout as we approach the gates.

"Visitors walking down the road," Knight shouts back.

"Are you sure they're not drunk and lost?" I counter.

"Take a look for yourself," Knight offers with a sweep of his hand once we get to the gates. I shine a flashlight on the two figures and my heart stops beating before picking up the pace again.

"Ouch." Kensi's sweet voice echoes through the darkness. "Do you mind asshole?" She shields her eyes from the light. I'm sure she doesn't know it's me because if she did, more than asshole would have flown from her lips.

"Kensi," I breathe and she stops in her tracks.

"Aftermath?"

"Yeah, Tiger, it's me." I turn to Knight still standing there with a dumb look on his face. "Open the fucking door," I demand.

Knight jumps and hits the button to roll the gates open. I want to sweep Kensi into my arms and kiss her. But I don't know what she'll do or how she'll react. Fuck it.

I approach father and daughter and take Kensi into my arms. Before she can protest, my lips are on hers. She stiffens from my touch, then melts into my arms, kissing me back. I groan against her lips, "God, I've missed you." My breath whispers across her skin.

"I've missed you too, but before we go any further we need to talk," Kensi responds, her fingers clutching onto my cut. I rest my forehead against hers, close my eyes and inhale her sweet scent.

"What happened?" Capone asks standing next to us. I don't let Kensi move so her dad answers for them.

Riding Through Life   J. Lynn Lombard

"I'd rather tell you inside instead of staying out here like sitting ducks. If they realized we escaped and know us, this is the first place they'll look. I won't put my daughter through that again." His blue eyes cut toward me, and I get the innuendo. He won't let anyone hurt her again unless it's over his dead body.

"Come on." Capone motions and we all follow him inside. I keep Kensi tucked under my arm, not letting her get away. The Ol' Ladies, kids, and bunnies are in bed so we don't have to worry about anyone bothering us. Once we're all inside, I notice the bruising and dried blood on the side of Kensi's head.

"Shit, what happened to you? Are you OK?" I ask, barely touching the side of her forehead. Kensi winces and pulls away.

"I'll be fine. I've dealt with worse." Her comment cuts me hard, but right now I deserve it.

"We were at my house when several men came storming in. I was restrained in the kitchen and could hear Kensi fighting with them out in the living room. She gave them a run for their money." Sheriff Donovan's eyes light up with admiration. "The one in charge knocked Kensi upside the head with the butt of his gun, stunning her and that's how they got the upper hand on us. I was already held at gunpoint and was forced to watch as they zip-tied my little girl up. When Kensi came too, they were moving us to the SUV. Then she passed out again and didn't wake up until we were at an apartment complex in the middle of nowhere. I knew

Riding Through Life   J. Lynn Lombard

how to get out of zip-ties so that's what I did while taking down the one guard they left with us.

"Once Kensi came too, she broke her zip-ties and we got out by the fire escape and headed here. I think Lil' Kay has a concussion. She's been throwing up and dizzy the whole walk here."

I take Kensi's face in my hands and carefully look her over. She's paler than normal and the mischievous sparkle in her multi-colored eyes is missing. "What can I get for you, Tiger? How can I make this better?"

It's a double-sided question and she hesitates. "I need answers." Kensi casts her eyes down to the floor and I gently lift her chin, making her look at me in the eyes.

"Do you want to do this here or in private?" I ask, giving her the option.

"Here, Aftermath. I can't focus on what happened to my dad and me until this thing between us is cleared." She shakes her head, holding back tears. "Even when my life was in jeopardy, the unanswered questions about us were running through my head."

"I swear on everything I am and the loyalty to you and my Club, I never touched that woman." Kensi doesn't say anything but continues to gaze into my eyes. "She came onto me when Red and I were at Nadia's dance studio. She walked up behind me, naked as the day her face came through her mother's crotch and tried to touch me. I got the fuck out of there and never looked back."

Riding Through Life J. Lynn Lombard

Kensi glances toward Red and he nods his head in confirmation. "What about the grocery store and the night of the party before you had to leave for the job? She told me everything, Aftermath. Every last detail of the two of you together. She even described the tattoo you got just for me." Kensi's eyes lower to the zipper of my jeans and I know what tattoo she's talking about. One night, I went to a tattoo shop in Vegas when we had to do a job for a woman Capone knows and got a tattoo of a Tiger on my junk. When it healed that was the best sex the two of us have ever shared.

My eyes shoot to Red, "Who is this fucking chick?" I'm pissed.

"I don't know, but I don't like it, brother. I'll start digging deeper." Red scurries off to his communications room.

"I swear, Kensi, I have never let that bitch touch me. Nor did I ever touch her. She came on to me at the grocery store with Pearl and Lexi, throwing out little jabs here and there. I didn't know how to handle it, so I told them to keep their mouths shut. Now I wish they didn't. And the night of the party, I couldn't stand looking at her skanky ass and I was exhausted. All I wanted was you in my bed and my arms without the drama. So, I went to our room and waited for you to get home. That way she couldn't corner me." I take Kensi's face gently in my hands and move as close as I can. "I swear you are the *only* woman I want or need. When you're not with me, I can't breathe. Say you believe me, Tiger, please."

Riding Through LifeJ. Lynn Lombard

"I believe you, Aftermath. I might be an idiot, but I can't breathe without you." I kiss Kensi with everything I have. All the love and adoration I have for this woman spills out of me and into her.

"I love you, Kensi Donovan. Will you still marry me? I might fuck up from time to time, but please knock me upside the head if I do. You're my everything and I want to ride through life with you by my side."

"Of course, I'll still marry you. You're my everything I want to ride through life with."

"Forever."

"And always."

"Thank fuck." Playboy groans. "He's been an inconsolable asshole on this whole trip."

I smile against Kensi's lips before I kiss her again.

"Not to be the other asshole, but we have to figure out who those men were that kidnapped you two," Capone speaks up.

"They said they were FBI," Kensi speaks up.

"I'll have Red check." Trigger states.

"Good idea and wake up Bones. He can work with Red." Capone orders.

"Do you think this bitch and those men who took us are working together?" Kensi asks.

"Why do you think that?" Capone asks.

"I don't know. With all the weird shit happening, I don't think it's a coincidence. What if she's a plant to try and get close to the Club while pushing me away from it and in return, my dad?"

Capone and the Sheriff pass a knowing look. Now that I'm in the loop I know what that look is for. Well, fuck me, it's not the Feds who are after Kensi and the Sheriff. If they're who I think they are, we're in some deep shit.

Riding Through Life   J. Lynn Lombard

Riding Through Life				J. Lynn Lombard

Chapter 15

Kensi

There's a slight chill in the air as I walk outside and head to the houses being built on the property. The structures form a semi-circle, with room to build more houses. It's spaced out enough to have a total of ten homes and will close off the center, making a complete circle. Capone and Danyella have the house closest to the Clubhouse, and Blayze and Monica are to their right. Torch, Daisy and the twins are to the left of Capone and Derange, Jezebelle and their daughter are next to Torch. Red and Nadia will be directly across from Capone in the circle. Aftermath and I have talked about building a house, but right now, all I want to do is get married.

It's been almost a month since those assholes kidnapped my dad and me. Red has been searching tirelessly with little results. Every time he has a lead, they disappear and our guards are up. The woman, Lynn, hasn't been seen since the night we escaped and my suspicion radar is pinging like crazy.

Aftermath and I are getting married in two days and the last thing I want is to have this looming over our day. Which is why I'm heading out to the homes being

Riding Through Life   J. Lynn Lombard

built. Trigger, Tiny, Dagger and the two prospects are out here and I need someone to take me to Nadia's dance studio without Aftermath or Red knowing about it. Red might not be able to find the bitch, but I know I can.

The closer I get to Capone's house, the louder the music and power tools are. I step through the French style front doors and gasp when I see how much is done. Cathedral ceilings are painted white, opening the space. Hardwood flooring is throughout the whole house, making my boots echo. I follow the music up the stairs and into the bedroom at the back. Trigger and Knight are cutting boards while Dagger and Seth are hanging them up. Tiny and his kitten are in the bathroom off of the bedroom.

"Trigger!" I shout over the noise. No one hears me, so I step closer and shout louder. "Trigger!" He still doesn't answer, so I grab a chunk of wood and toss it at him. It hits him square in the chest.

"What the fuck!" Trigger jumps in the middle of cutting and glares around the room until his gaze lands on me trying not to laugh. "You're an asshole, scaring me like that."

"Sorry." I shrug my shoulders. Not really sorry and thought it was pretty funny.

"What do you need, Kensi?" Trigger asks, irritation dripping from him.

"I need a ride."

"So, get Aftermath to give you a ride." Trigger counters.

Riding Through Life　　　　　　　　J. Lynn Lombard

　　　I knew this was going to be tough, but damn, he isn't giving me any room. "I can't have Aftermath give me a ride."

　　　"Can't help, sorry." Trigger goes back to cutting the board when I fling another chunk of wood at him. "Fuck."

　　　"I need a ride, Trigger." I plead.

　　　"No."

　　　"Yes."

　　　"No."

　　　Gah! He's driving me nuts. "Then have Seth or Knight take me. But I need a damn ride."

　　　"Why?" Trigger asks.

　　　"Because I have to get something for Aftermath before our wedding and since I'm getting married in two days, I have to get it now. But you can't tell him I left. It's a surprise." I add in before he calls Aftermath. The partial lie rolls off my tongue and I feel guilty for lying to Trigger, but I have no choice, not if I want to take this bitch down.

　　　Trigger scrubs his hands down his bearded face. "Fuck. I'm going to regret this but Knight, take her where she needs to go. Nowhere else."

　　　"Yes, sir," Knight answers, dropping his piece of wood.

Riding Through Life   J. Lynn Lombard

"And if she wants to go elsewhere," Trigger points at me like I always cause trouble. "Bring her back here."

"Anything else?" Knight asks.

"Don't let her out of your sight. She's been known to get into trouble or trouble finds her." Trigger responds.

"I won't."

"Good, now get before I change my mind." Knight and I start to walk out before Trigger stops me. "Kensi, I will give you one hour to get your ass back here. If you're not here, I will let Aftermath know. If this is a fucking trick, I will let Aftermath know then he can deal with your ass."

I pull Knight out of the bedroom by his arm before Trigger changes his mind. Knight is Daisy's twin brother she didn't know about until their grandfather who was the Prime Minister of Ireland kidnapped Daisy and was holding Knight captive with lies and brainwashing. Knight stopped believing their grandfather and when the Royal Bastards came to Daisy's rescue, Knight helped them retrieve her and Bones who was kidnapped and beaten with Daisy. Since then, Daisy and Knight have been close and he moved here to prospect for the Royal Bastards. Knight is a very handsome guy with short blonde hair, a light stubble on his face, and piercing blue eyes. He's muscular in all the right places like most of these guys but he isn't big like Aftermath or Tiny. He has a skinny but muscular look about him and he stands just a few inches taller than my five-foot-six frame.

Riding Through Life   J. Lynn Lombard

    I've been around the Club for a while now and these guys need a break. If it's not one thing it's another they've gone through, so if I can take care of this bitch on my own and give them a break, then that's what I'll do, no matter what the consequences are.

    "Damn, you're in a rush," Knight says pulling away from me.

    "Yeah, I am. If I don't get out of here soon, Trigger will change his mind about letting you go with me and call Aftermath. This is really important, Knight." I lay it on thick, hoping Knight bites.

    "Fine." Knight releases a deep sigh. "I have a feeling I'm going to regret this."

    I get in on the passenger side of his maroon Dodge Charger and Knight slides into the driver's side. He fires it up and the engine barks before settling into a steady purr. He pulls out of his parking spot and the gates slide open, allowing us through. Once we hit the gravel road, Knight guns the gas, shooting us onto the road.

    "Where are we going?" Knight asks, shifting gears.

    "Keep driving and I'll tell you where to turn." If I tell him now, he will turn this bitch around and that's the last thing I want to do.

    We head south on the PCH and I tell him to exit. Giving him a few directions, we pull into Nadia's dance

Riding Through Life   J. Lynn Lombard

studio. It's locked up tight, but I lifted the key from Nadia before I left and I know the passcode.

Knight parks the car and looks at me with a quirked eyebrow. "What are we doing here?"

I climb out, "Stay out here I'll only be a minute." I slam the door on a curse flowing from Knight's lips and jog to the door. Once I reach the door, I enter the passcode and unlock the front door. Walking inside, silence greets me, putting me on edge. I make sure to lock the door behind me so Knight can't get in.

I step quietly into the plush carpet and head down the hallway toward the dance floor. Once that is clear, I check every room that branches off until I'm satisfied no one is here with me. Then I make my way back down the hallway toward the locker rooms. Since Lynn doesn't have an office and only a locker, I head into the locker room. I don't know which one is hers, but from what Aftermath told me, she should be near the door. At least I hope her locker is.

I check the room to make sure no one is in here and then I begin looking through each locker. For the ones that are locked, I pick the lock and rummage through. I have to be quick but thorough because if Red is alerted someone is here, it'll be a matter of moments before he tells Aftermath and Aftermath comes to get me.

Searching each locker in here in every row, I come up empty handed. Well, shit. Maybe Nadia fired her and she took all her shit. If that's the case, I'll never find her. I slam the last locker shut and lean against it. This was a wasteful trip.

Riding Through Life   J. Lynn Lombard

"Shit." I hit my palm on the locker door and it echoes through the open room. I exit and head to the front door. Standing in front of the door in all his menacing glory is the man who makes my heart skip a beat and desire to thrum through my body. I shiver when his dark gaze lands on me.

"Shit," I whisper under my breath. Aftermath must have known what I said because he smirks and crooks his finger. I unlock the door and lock it up behind me, playing it casually. "What's up, Aftermath?" I ask, leaning against the door. Even though my heart is pounding against my rib cage, I appear relaxed on the outside, like this is an everyday occurrence.

"What's up?" Aftermath's deep voice grows deeper and more menacing with every word he takes. "What's up? How about I get an alert on my phone that your ass left the property but that couldn't be true. You promised you'd stay put and not go anywhere alone."

"I'm not alone," I straighten my spine. "I have Knight with me."

Aftermath's deadly smirk raises the hair on my arm. "Oh, he'll be dealt with." Aftermath steps closer, caging my body against the door. His nose trails down the side of my face to the column of my neck. His hot breath whispers across my skin, making me lose my train of thought. "Get your sexy ass on the back of my bike, Tiger. You have a punishment coming your way." His tongue snakes out, as his plump lips suck on the spot that drives me wild.

Riding Through Life J. Lynn Lombard

"Wait," I say holding up my hands. Aftermath steps back but not enough to let me think straight, just enough where I can look into his dark gaze. "It's not Knight's fault. I refused to tell him where I wanted to go."

"Tiger, Knight knew the moment he took off with you, he'd be in trouble, no matter what you think you told him to do." Aftermath's hot breath fans across my neck making me shiver. "Since he had Trigger's permission, I'll go easy on him, but he isn't getting away with leaving with you."

Aftermath kisses his way from my neck up to my lips. Once his lips land on mine, I don't hold back. I kiss him with everything I have. When we break apart, I'm crazy with desire and can't control my filter. "I'm sorry, Aftermath. I wanted…"

Aftermath kisses me again, halting my rambling. He pulls away and rests his forehead against mine. "I know what you wanted to do, Tiger, but you can't always ride off to save the day. Trust me when I say this bitch will get what's coming to her. We've got it handled."

"I'm sorry."

"What if something happened to you? What if that chick was in there and you locked your only form of protection out? What if she killed you while you were playing detective? Then I'd be either sitting in prison or a grave right next to you." Aftermath cups my cheeks. "You are more important than that bitch. Your life means so much more than hers. Please, for the love of God and all that is holy, stop getting yourself into these situations. One of these days, I'm afraid I won't make it to you in time."

"Shit, I didn't think of it that way. Now I really feel like shit." I'd slap my forehead if Aftermath wasn't crowding my space.

"I wasn't telling you this to make you stop being who you are, Kensi. I'm telling you this so you are aware of what could happen. I don't want you to change, just be more cautious of the decisions you make. You're the only woman who flips my world upside down and can bring me peace."

"You say the sweetest things." I lean in and press my lips to Aftermath's. "I'll try to be better at my decisions."

"That's all I ask. I don't have any helmets so we're riding illegally for a while." Aftermath picks me up and I wrap my legs around his waist, his hardness pressing into my core and I moan. "You're going to be the death of me, woman."

"Nah, I'll be your saving grace," I respond.

Aftermath sets me on his bike and then climbs on in front of me. He fires his girl up and the rumble is soothing. "Hang tight and don't let go."

I rest my head on Aftermath's back and tightly wrap my arms around his waist. "I'll never let you go again," I vow.

Riding Through Life		J. Lynn Lombard

Riding Through Life		J. Lynn Lombard

Chapter 16

Kensi

"C'mon, Kensi! We're going to be late!" Nadia shouts from behind my closed door.

I grumble and lay my naked body across Aftermath's. Today is the eve of our wedding and the girls want to take me out to a bachelorette party while the guys are taking Aftermath to his bachelor party. "Do we have to go? I'd rather stay in bed with you all night until we say I do tomorrow."

I straddle Aftermath's naked body and kiss him deeply. His hardness nudging my entrance. All I have to do is shift just right and he'll be buried inside of me. We break apart and I'm ready for the next round.

"That does sound like a fantastic idea. I can carry you down the aisle with my dick still inside of you and pound into you while the preacher says our vows." Aftermath slaps my ass, making me shift. He's pressing into my entrance, but not enough to slip inside yet.

I think about that and my eyes widen. "You wouldn't!"

Riding Through Life   J. Lynn Lombard

"I would if it's what my Tiger wants."

"But Dagger is performing our ceremony! I can't do that to him!" I sit up and Aftermath slips inside of me, finally. "Uh!" I moan, tipping my head back. "If it gets you this hard, maybe exhibition wouldn't be so bad." I rock on top of Aftermath, hitting all the right places.

Aftermath sits up, "This body is for my eyes only. I'll rip anyone's eyes out and feed it to them if they look at you like this." Aftermath flips us over and he drives deep and hard. Before I know it, I'm reaching my peak and Aftermath follows shortly after.

We shower together and please each other one more time before we face the music and a pissed-off Nadia and Red. We're well over an hour late leaving.

"It's about fucking time!" Nadia throws her hands up. "You're lucky Grace is a godsend with children or I wouldn't be going anywhere." Aftermath's mom, Grace aka Silver Grace, agreed to watch all the club kids tonight with Bones and Seth so the Club could go out and celebrate.

Nadia grabs my arm and pulls. "Hold on, Nadia. Why the rush?" I ask, releasing her grip from my arm.

"Because the longer I'm here and not holding Matthew, the guiltier I feel. If I'm far enough away, I won't feel as guilty." Nadia brushes the tears from her eyes.

"Shit. Now I feel like an asshole for making you wait." I respond.

Riding Through Life   J. Lynn Lombard

"Good, then let's go." Nadia shakes off the sadness and pulls me again.

"Tiger." One word from Aftermath has both Nadia and me stopping. I turn to face him. Aftermath stalks toward us. "Stay out of trouble tonight, please." He cups my face and delivers a panty-melting kiss.

"I'll do my best," I respond breathlessly. That's the best I can do. Trouble always finds me even when I'm not looking for it.

Aftermath releases my cheeks and Nadia pulls me out the door of the Clubhouse and into the car. She's freakishly strong for being a tiny dancer. Nadia climbs into the driver's seat, starts the car and takes off. The gates are already open for us so she doesn't even have to stop. Once we get on the road, Nadia cranks the music up and we sing and dance on the way to my bachelorette party.

"We're here!" Nadia's excitement is rubbing off on me. "This place has the top-of-the-line entertainment suited for everyone."

I look out the front window and my jaw drops. "You realize this is a strip club right?" I ask.

"No, silly. The dancers on stage don't get naked. It's a burlesque club. Some of my dancers perform here and they made a special skit and dance in your honor tonight." Nadia opens her door but I'm still hesitant. "Come on, the rest of the ladies are already inside."

Riding Through Life   J. Lynn Lombard

I inhale a deep breath, praying I don't fuck this night up and trouble doesn't come knocking on my door. Exhaling, I open my car door and slam it shut behind me. Nadia wraps her arm around mine. "That's my girl! You only get married once and tonight we're going out in style!"

The bouncer at the door opens it for us, "Have a great night, ladies."

"Thanks!" Nadia beams him with a smile and I swear he fell to the ground in worship. All this woman has to do is bat her sultry eyes at a man and he falls to her feet. But luckily for her, she has Red who is her everything. Those men don't stand a chance against Nadia's blushing biker.

We make it inside and the room is dark except for the stage. Men and women are doing some kind of skit, making the patrons laugh with their sexual innuendos. Nadia leads me to a larger corner table to the right of the stage. The dark oak and black and gold chairs take up half of the room but still gives us privacy from the other patrons and we're close enough to the stage without being disruptive.

Danyella, Monica, Jezebelle, Daisy, Exleigh, Syvannah and Pearl are all sitting in the booth, chatting, drinking and having a fun time.

They all squeal when they see us and Danyella hugs me first while slapping a tiara on my head. "For the soon-to-be Mrs. Jacobs!"

The girls cheer and then Monica comes up with a sash that reads I'm the crazy bride. She places it over

Riding Through Life   J. Lynn Lombard

my head and giggles. Then Daisy comes to me, holding a pair of sunglasses in her hands. She plops them on my face and hugs me.

Next Jezebelle comes up to me with a whip and handcuffs. I raise an eyebrow and she shrugs. "You can never have too many."

Once we take our seats, a man in tight leather shorts and a red bow tie greets us. "Ladies, what can I get you tonight? Remember, the bride drinks for free here." He gives me a wink and looks me up and down. His voice is deep and sexual and his eyes are baby blue. Pearl fans herself while checking our waiter out.

"Damn, where have you been all my life?" Pearl's husky voice captures our waiter's attention.

"Baby, I've been here ready to serve you fine ladies." We all cheer, while he winks at Pearl and I swear there are hearts in her eyes. But I know better, she has a thing for Tiny, who only uses her when he needs to take the edge off. She lets him so it's not my business what she wants to do and with whom.

I give the waiter our drink orders and he saunters off, putting a flirtatious sway in his hips. He knows how to use what his mama gave him and for that, he'll get great tips tonight.

After chatting and drinking for a while, I'm starting to feel tipsy but don't let it stop me from having fun. The dancers on stage are wearing beautiful black corsets with glittery sequins, black gloves made from the same material, stockings, black heels and a black top

Riding Through Life   J. Lynn Lombard

hat. Each time they move, the sequins glitter under the lights. Each dance they perform is sensual and beautiful, not tacky. The slow jazz they're dancing to mesmerizes each person and pulls them into the dance they're performing. Their dance entrances me so much that I don't notice we have more people sitting at our table. Not until strong hands grip my waist and pull me onto his lap.

"Is that turning you on, Tiger?" Aftermath growls into my ear and sends chills down my spine. Already turned on and tipsy, all rational thoughts leave my head as I lean into Aftermath. His strong hands roam up and down my sides while his breath heats my skin.

"Hmm…" I answer. Turning in his lap so my legs are straddling Aftermath's hips, we're groin to groin and I can feel his erection pressing against me. I slowly dance to the music surrounding us, grinding and moving against him. Aftermath groans and presses his hips into mine on each thrust. It's intimate and intoxicating. Once the song is finished, I lean into Aftermath, pressing my lips to his.

"Whew, I need a cold shower after that show." Nadia fans her face.

My face turns red from embarrassment and I try to move off Aftermath's lap, but he tightens his grip on my hips. "You're not going anywhere, Tiger."

"I have to use the bathroom, Aftermath." I wink and his sexy deep laugh penetrates my soul.

Riding Through Life   J. Lynn Lombard

"Ok, Tiger, but if you're not back here in ten minutes, I'm coming to get you." Aftermath nips the sensitive skin on my neck before releasing me.

"Make it five and you have a deal." Nadia, Danyella and I head toward the bathrooms at the back of the club.

Aftermath chuckles darkly, his intense gaze watching me walk away. I put an extra sway in my hips, knowing it drives him crazy. The three of us do our business and head back to our table.

"Thank you, ladies," I say putting my arms around Danyella and Nadia's waists. "You have made this night fantastic and I appreciate everything you've done for me."

"I wish I knew what was happening between the two of you when you left," Nadia responds, putting her arm around me. "I tried to call you several times but it kept going to voicemail and Red wouldn't give me any answers."

"Same here. I don't know what was wrong with your phone or if it was ours but none of my texts or calls would go through to you." Danyella reiterates. "We tried for a few days and any time we asked, Capone would say everything was fine and not to worry." Danyella snorts. "Weren't they wrong? I'll bet they will never make the mistake of brushing us off again."

"Everything was fine until the third day. I was getting messages, just not from any of you." I stop walking, halting Nadia and Danyella. "Do you think that bitch had anything to do with it?" Shaking my head, I continue. "There's no way she's a petty dancer. How would she have the ability to block my phone from incoming messages or calls except from her."

"Wait," Danyella looks around before speaking. "You were getting messages from her?" She whisper shouts.

"Yeah. That's how I found out all the misinformation I had about her and Aftermath. It still boils my blood knowing I believed her lies. When no one else reached out, I thought it was true, but I should have known better."

"Well, it's all in the past and she's going to stay there." Nadia squeezes my shoulders. "I fired her and kicked her ass out the door. If she shows up, I'll gladly do it again. No one fucks with my best friend."

"Here, here!" Danyella chants.

We walk back to our table and I stop dead in my tracks. Aftermath is at the bar, getting more drinks and next to him is none other than Lynn, nursing a drink. Her blonde hair is piled high on top of her head and she's doing whatever she can to get Aftermath's attention. He keeps brushing her off but she is still trying. She's wearing the sluttiest clothes I've ever seen and I've been around plenty of Patch Bunnies and strippers. Her boobs are close to popping out of a skimpy pink tank top and her v-jay is practically kissing the floor in the shortest skirt I've ever seen. Her heels will trip over it if she moves.

Riding Through Life   J. Lynn Lombard

Having enough of Lynn's bullshit, I release Nadia and Danyella and head straight for her. I clock her upside the head, knocking the slut off her stool before she even sees me coming. Lynn tries standing up, but I knock her back down with a kick to the stomach. All the rage, anger and frustration built up inside of me comes rushing out.

I straddle her chest and begin raining blow after blow on her face and body. She pulls my hair and claws at my arms, but I don't stop. Not until a strong set of arms yanks me up. I kick and fight with whoever has a hold of me, kicking Lynn in the face in the process.

"Tiger, put your claws away." Aftermath demands. His grip is strong and commanding around my waist. I finally stop fighting, all the adrenaline leaves my body.

"Shit." I groan.

"Shit is right. We've got to get out of here." Aftermath explains.

As soon as the words leave his lips, the police come barging in with their guns drawn. The dancers stop what they're doing, the lights are turned up and the patrons are all watching and waiting to see what happens next.

"Get on the ground, now!" One officer demands, pointing his gun at me and Aftermath. Everything is happening so fast, I don't have time to process anything. I'm on the ground being handcuffed and hauled to my feet. Aftermath is being detained on the other side of the room along with the rest of the Royal Bastards. They look like caged animals pacing back and forth, waiting for an opportunity to attack.

"I want her arrested for aggravated assault!" Lynn screeches from her stool. "She attacked me!" She whines.

"And I'll do it again, bitch. Fuck with me and you'll regret it." I spit out.

"That's enough, Miss Donovan." The officer holding me replies, shifting my arms up higher so I can't move. "You have the right to remain silent. Anything you say can and will be held against you in a court of law."

I tune the arresting officer out. I've been through it before and I know the drill. Craning my neck toward Aftermath on the other side of the room, I shout. "I'm sorry, Aftermath. I love you."

"I love you, Tiger. Don't worry, we'll get you out." Aftermath shouts back.

The arresting officer hauls me out the door and into the back of his car. Within fifteen minutes, I'm sitting in a jail cell, alone. I've really screwed up this time. I'm supposed to be getting married tomorrow, not sitting in a jail cell up shit's creek without a paddle. But then again, it wouldn't be me if trouble didn't find me.

I hope Aftermath can pull through and get me out before we're supposed to get married tomorrow.

Chapter 17

Aftermath

"Fuck!" I slam my fist on the table, shaking it from the force while I watch Kensi being hauled away in handcuffs. When she's out of my sight, I start pacing, agitation thrumming over my skin. The buzz I had from drinking earlier evaporates, leaving a pounding headache in its wake.

"Easy, brother. If you get arrested, you won't be able to help her." Capone rests his palm on my shoulder, holding me in my seat.

My body vibrates with rage when I lock eyes on Lynn who is talking to an officer. She flashes him with a seductive smile and adjusts her top so her chest is more exposed. Her eyes land on me and she smirks, giving me a wink. What the actual fuck? Is this chick psycho or something? I stand, ready to attack the bitch when Capone and Blayde stand in front of me, blocking me from going after her.

"Not right now, Aftermath. Now we have her details and justice will be delivered for fucking with one of our own." Blayze puts his hands on my chest, keeping me back. "Let Red do his thing and then we can get Kensi out."

"Fuck!" I growl, scrubbing my hands down my face in agitation. "We're supposed to get married tomorrow and we can't do that with Kensi locked up."

"We're going to give them some time to get her processed and you to sober up then we'll go to the precinct and see what we have to do to get her out. Right now, I need you to stay calm and level-headed."

"I am sober but I can't just sit here and do nothing!" I shout, throwing my hands up in the air.

"You're not doing nothing, you're leaning on your brothers in a time of need. Suck it up and take the fucking help." Capone demands shoving me into my chair.

I sit with a hard thud, my weight making it groan in protest. I rest my elbows on the table and rest my head in my hands. "What can we do?" I ask quietly.

"Red has already left with Nadia. When he gets to the Clubhouse, he's going to get Bones and the three of them will do what they can to get her out. Until then, you need to remain calm. Once Knight gets here, he's taking the rest of the girls home along with Torch, Blayze and Derange. Then the rest of us will head to the jail and see what we can do." Capone calmly relays what's going to happen and it makes me calm as well.

"Fine, but I won't let a little badge stop me from marrying Kensi tomorrow," I grumble.

Riding Through Life   J. Lynn Lombard

Lynn smiles at the police officer while running her fingernail down his chest. She bats her eyes at him and my stomach rolls. I stand up from the table, anger radiating through my body at the nerve of this woman.

"Where the hell are you going?" Capone demands.

"To the bathroom, if that's alright with you, Prez," I respond, not keeping the snarky attitude out of my voice.

"Fine, but don't do anything stupid," Capone acknowledges.

I head for the back of the club but instead of going into the bathroom, I shoulder my way out the back door. Once I'm standing outside, I inhale the crisp night air deep into my lungs. My head clears a little more and I stare up at the sky, wishing this night had gone differently. Kensi is always finding trouble, or trouble always finds her, but I wouldn't change her for the world.

Pulling out my phone, I begin to pace. I need to call her dad and let him know what happened. I dial his number and take a deep breath before putting my phone up to my ear.

"Something's happened to Kensi." Sheriff Donavan states, picking up the phone on the second ring. He knows if his phone rings this late at night, it's nothing good and it has everything to do with Kensi.

Riding Through Life   J. Lynn Lombard

"Kensi has been arrested and I don't know if I can get her out before tomorrow." I relay what happened tonight and can feel the tension coming from the other line.

"What the actual fuck?" The good Sheriff swears out loud. "Tomorrow is her wedding day, Aftermath. What are we going to do?"

"I don't know, but I'm working on it. I wanted to update you so this didn't come as a surprise."

"I might be able to pull some strings. Sit tight and wait for my call." Sheriff Donovan hangs up the phone before I can respond.

My woman is sitting in a jail cell, probably scared out of her mind and Donovan wants me to sit tight. Is he fucking crazy? Capone wants me to wait. Is he fucking crazy too? I'm not sitting here with my thumb up my ass. I'm going to get my woman out, even if I have to break her out of jail.

Riding my bike through the city, I wonder how long it will take before Capone realizes I left. I can't just sit back and let my Tiger rot in a jail cell for standing up for me. Something weird is going on with that Lynn chick and hopefully Red or Bones can get to the bottom of it quickly.

I pull into the precinct, expecting Capone or one of my brothers to anticipate my next move and waiting for me, but they're not. I turn off my bike and set the kickstand down. Climbing off my bike, I stow any weapons I have and lock up the saddle bags. I don't need any unnecessary charges against me. I leave my cut on

Riding Through Life   J. Lynn Lombard
and head for the double glass doors. I've never been inside here willingly before so this is something new.

I step inside and the fluorescent lights against the white tile flooring hurt my eyes and I have to blink a couple of times to adjust. The scent of bleach and floor cleaner assaults my nose and I hold back a sneeze.

In front of me are steps that lead up to a big oak desk full of paperwork, a computer, a phone and various shit you'd find in a police station. A grumpy-looking man with a wrinkled uniform and salt and pepper hair stands behind the desk watching me as I take in my surroundings and walk his way.

"Can I help you?" he asks, eyeing me wearily.

"I hope so. My Ol' Lady was brought in earlier and I want to know how I can get her out," I answer, leaving the edge out of my voice with how uncomfortable I am.

He raises a bushy eyebrow, "Name?"

"Kensi Donovan," I answer, looking around. Police officers are coming and going and a few keep watching me like they're waiting for me to do something. Jesus, judgmental or what? One officer in particular is standing down the hallway, watching me. He looks familiar but I can't place where I know him from.

"I'm not seeing a Kensi Donovan in the system. Are you sure they brought her here?" The officer asks.

Riding Through Life   J. Lynn Lombard

"Positive. The alleged incident happened over on West and Turner."

"Let me check another database, hold on a sec." He types a few keys before grunting. "Found her, she is being processed for aggravated assault on a civilian."

"Alleged assault," I say pointedly.

"Once she is processed, then she will go in front of a judge on Monday and get her bail set. Sorry, but there is nothing that can be done until the court opens Monday morning. And since it's a Holiday weekend, you won't be able to get ahold of anyone until then anyway."

The one officer watching me with his hand resting on his holster the whole time smirks. His grip shifts to pull his gun out when I stare back at him. "Can I fucking help you?" I ask, sick of his judgmental shit.

"Yeah, you can turn around and walk out before you find yourself in trouble." He responds.

I snort, "In trouble for what? I didn't do shit."

"That's what you think. Do you think it's ok to cheat on your woman with another? Then let your woman beat the shit out of the woman you cheated on her with without doing anything to stop her?" Aggravation is rolling off him in waves.

"What the fuck are you ragging about?" My temper is on a short fuse and this motherfucker just lit it up.

"I heard all about it from the victim. In my opinion, you should be locked up behind bars instead of that innocent woman." He steps closer, his face a deep shade of red and I spot the Sheriff's badge pinned to his chest.

That's why he looks familiar. He was the Sheriff who took the psychopath's statement. "Is that what she's telling everyone? I cheated on my fiancée with that skank?" I bark out a laugh and turn my back on the Sheriff, directing my attention back to the guy behind the desk. "Can I at least see her? We're supposed to be getting married tomorrow." I plead.

"I'm sorry, but no visitors this late at night. You'll have to come back tomorrow." The officer behind the desk flicks his gaze at the Sheriff coming up behind me.

"Touch me and I will rip out your arms and beat you with them." I threaten. I listen while still watching the desk officer and the short-tempered one doesn't disappoint. I turn to face him. He stands directly behind me, his chest puffed out like he's someone special. Well, shit. I guess if I can't visit with my Tiger, I might as well join her.

Shrugging, I step forward and slam my forehead into short temper's nose. Blood instantly starts spilling down his face. Might as well go for broke. "How'd you like that motherfucker." I punch him in the stomach, making him bend over wheezing. "I never touched that skank and as for Kensi doing what she allegedly did, that skank got everything she deserved." I hit him one more time before I'm being dragged off the asshole by four men. Two on each arm, holding me up. Short Temper Sheriff straightens the best he can before he wipes the blood from his face. He steps up to me and I spit in his face.

"What's the matter? Can't take me on, on your own? Have to have others help?" I taunt. "That's why you're a weasel dick..." My words trail off as red-hot pain laces my body and locks up my muscles. I shake while every fiber of my being loses control with intense electrical pain that can't compare to anything I've ever felt before.

I'm thrown onto the ground face first and handcuffed before I have all my faculties back. Well, that's the first for me. Fucking tased in a police station.

"You have the right to remain silent. Anything you say or do can and will be used against you in a court of law." The Sheriff drones on. I've heard it before tons of times so I pass out from the pain while I'm being booked.

Fuck it. If I can't get Kensi out, I might as well join her.

Riding Through Life   J. Lynn Lombard

Chapter 18

Kensi

I cannot believe this is happening! On the night before my wedding day, I had to lose my cool and hit the bitch. Even though she deserved everything she got, I should have restrained myself until after Aftermath and I were married.
"Shit!" I growl, punching the pillow.

I'm in a single jail cell kind of like the ones you find in the small-town area, like on The Andy Griffith Show or some shit. There is no one else here besides me and I'm bored out of my mind. The officer on duty is napping at his desk, with his feet propped up. They haven't given me my one phone call yet and that is pissing me off. I'm lying on a hard cement slab with a piece of plastic underneath me as a mattress and a flat-ass pillow for my head. The blanket they gave me is flimsy like my pillow, scratchy, and doesn't hold any warmth.

At least they let me keep my clothes on instead of wearing a prison-issued orange jumpsuit. "What am I going to do now? There's no way they'll let me out of

Riding Through Life   J. Lynn Lombard

here." I say out loud. I'm so bored, I'm talking to myself out loud.

A loud crash and shouting erupts behind the thick door before an officer opens it. I sit up and watch with morbid curiosity. One officer holds the door open while four more drag a man through it. Two officers are under one arm, while the other two are under his other arm. Once the officer holding the door open steps out of the way, I gasp.

"Aftermath! No!" I shout, moving to the bars of my cell. I grip the cold steel and try to shake it. They're dragging his big body in by the armpits. He isn't fighting back. The one officer napping on his desk stands up quickly and unlocks the cell next to me. The four guards toss Aftermath in like a sack of potatoes and quickly close the door before locking it.

"What's going on? Why is he in here?" I ask, shouting to be heard.

The Sheriff with blood dripping down his nose snarls at me, "Your boyfriend thought it'd be smart to headbutt me." He wipes blood from his nose before continuing. "Is this how you like to be treated? Letting him walk all over you and cheating on you with an innocent woman then letting you get arrested?"

I laugh. I full blown belly laugh. I laugh so hard tears roll down my face and I can't breathe. Once I gain control again, I take a deep breath and stand up straight staring right into this asshole's eyes. "You're an idiot." I snort. "Aftermath didn't cheat on me. Lynn is a liar and a manipulator who deserves everything she has coming for her." I deliver this with such vehement fury, that the

Riding Through Life   J. Lynn Lombard

Sheriff takes a step back. "If you believe her sad excuse as to why she tripped over my feet and landed on my fists, then you need to have a reality check." I sit on my concrete slab while they lock Aftermath up. He is starting to move and I exhale a relieved breath.

I stare into the dickhead's eyes. "Leave. Unless you want to apologize to me, I suggest you get the fuck out of here. You obviously don't know who you're messing with."

He breaks eye contact first and stomps back out the door they dragged Aftermath through. The officer who was sleeping at his desk looks conflicted about what to do.

I make eye contact with him. "You can either get the fuck out too or give me my one phone call," I demand. He doesn't respond, he just stares at me with his mouth opening and closing several times like a fish out of water. He's tall with short-cropped brown hair and piercing blue eyes. I roll my eyes and stand up. Crossing my jail cell, I grab hold of the bars and lean into them as far as I can go. "What's got your tongue tied?" I ask, batting my eyes and using my best seductive voice. A voice that usually gets me whatever I want.

"I...he...you...they...," the officer stutters and then shakes his head. "Do you know who that is? How dangerous he is?" He whispers the last part, baffled I went toe to toe with the local Sheriff.

I crook my finger, asking the officer to come closer. He does, still mystified by what I said. Once he's close enough for me to whisper I answer. "I know exactly who he is and he won't do a damn thing about this. Do you know why?" He shakes his head. "Because I'm Kensi Donovan and my father is Special Agent Zachary Donovan, FBI."

I smile smugly before walking away from the bars and sitting on my concrete slab. "So, Officer Daniels, if you let me make my one phone call, I will make sure you don't get on the FBI's bad side, or you continue to deny me, and you'll go down with Sheriff Long."

Aftermath groans before turning over. I spring from my bed and land on my knees next to the bars separating us. "Aftermath, are you OK?" I ask through the lump in my throat.

"That was the sexiest thing I've heard since the moment you were arrested, Tiger." Aftermath's voice is husky and desire floods my core.

"What are you doing here, you big beast?" I grip the bars tighter, wishing I could be in Aftermath's arms.

"Well, Tiger, I took a page out of your book. Figured if they won't let me in to visit you, I'd join you." Aftermath sits up and shuffles his big body toward the bars separating us. "And for future recommendations, do not get tased. That shit hurts like a bitch."

I giggle and lean my head against the bars. Aftermath does the same while threading his arms through the bars to hold me the best he can. "I love you, Aftermath."

"I love you, too, Kensi."

Riding Through Life   J. Lynn Lombard

"I'm sorry I ruined our wedding." I sniffle, holding back tears. "If that skank didn't show up, I'd be doing my own private dance for you. This is all my fault."

Aftermath kisses the top of my head through the bars. It's not comfortable, but it's what we have right now. "Nothing is ruined, Tiger, and it's not your fault. Just a little delayed for the time being but let's not think about that right now. All I want to do is hold my beautiful bride-to-be until we get released and from what the guy at the desk told me, it won't be until Monday."

"Then let's get comfy." I pull away and grab my blanket, flat-ass pillow and mattress and drag it to the bars. Aftermath does the same and we make our little nest with bars separating us.

"For the love of all that is holy." Officer Daniels grumbles from his desk. He stands up, grabs the set of keys hanging on a ring and walks toward us. "If either of you gets any bad ideas about overpowering me or end up fucking in here, I will separate the two of you and you won't like the repercussions." He unlocks my cell and slides it back, making a loud clinking noise. "Come on. I don't have all night."

Aftermath and I stand up and I tentatively step outside my cell. I'm hesitant, thinking this is some kind of trap and I'll get more charges thrown on me, but Officer Daniels unlocks Aftermath's cell and motions for me to get in. I step inside with my blankets and pillow and Daniels closes the cell behind me.

Riding Through Life   J. Lynn Lombard

I turn around, "Wait. What if Sheriff Long comes back? Won't you get into trouble?"

"Kensi, if Sheriff Long comes back, Hell will freeze over. It's a Holiday weekend, his sorry ass won't be back until Tuesday, maybe Wednesday, not even if this place was burning to the ground. I'm on duty all weekend so it's just the three of us. Get comfortable, it's going to be a while." Officer Daniels assures.

Aftermath wraps his big arms around me and I lean into him, inhaling his intoxicating scent. Officer Daniels saunters back to his desk and grabs his cell phone. He walks back to us and hands it to me through the bars. "One phone call for each of you and then hand it back. I know RBMC are a good bunch of outlaw bikers so don't betray my faith in your Club."

I take the phone and Officer Daniels walks away. I quickly find the call icon and dial my dad's number. After three rings, his gruff voice comes across the line. "Sheriff Donovan speaking."

"Dad?" I croak. My body fills with relief hearing his voice.

"Lil' Kay? How are you calling me? What's going on?" Concern laces his tone.

"Dad, listen. I don't have a lot of time, but what I'm going to tell you, I need you to relay to Capone. Do you remember when you did some research on a man named Long?"

"Yeah," he hesitates. We don't talk about this over the phone, ever, but it needs to be done this time.

Riding Through Life   J. Lynn Lombard

"Long is the one who arrested me."

"What!" Dad shouts from the other end of the phone. "That motherfucker is going down. If he thinks for one minute he can..."

"Dad, stop." I interrupt him. I don't want him to say too much and have Aftermath overhear. As far as I know, he doesn't know about my dad's side business. I've been telling him to pull the Royal Bastards in, but he's a stubborn one. "I'm not alone. Aftermath is right next to me."

"How the hell did that happen?" He gruffly replies.

"Let's say Long and a taser doesn't like my man."

"After I broke his nose," Aftermath chimes in.

"Wait, are you two with each other?" Dad asks.

"Yes, Officer Daniels put us together," I answer.

"OK, sit tight, the two of you. I have to do something I swore I'd never do again, but I don't see how to get you out of this." The determination in his voice has the little hairs on the back of my neck rise.

"Dad, no. Call Capone and tell him what's happening, please. He will be expecting your call. If you do what I think you're doing, I will murder you myself," I respond. It's cryptic but there is no way I'm letting my dad sacrifice his freedom for mine.

"OK, Lil' Kay, I'll do this your way for now. But if it doesn't work, I will do it my way."

Riding Through Life   J. Lynn Lombard

"Thank you, Dad. I love you."

"Love you, too, Lil' Kay. Sit tight and we'll figure out a way to get you two out."

I hang up the phone and fight back tears of relief. Handing the phone to Aftermath, I put our blankets and pillows on the floor, making a nifty little pallet bed while he talks to Capone. I don't listen in on his conversation, letting him have his privacy for *Club business*.

Once Aftermath is done, he sets the phone outside the bars for Officer Daniels to retrieve and he wraps his arms around me, pulling my back to his front. Aftermath gently kisses the side of my neck, making my legs shake with need. His arousal is hard against my backside but I'm not going to jeopardize our luck.

For hours we just either lay down and cuddle or stand and hold each other tight. Neither one of us saying much but we both know we are weathering this storm together and will come out stronger on the other side.

Riding Through Life   J. Lynn Lombard

Chapter 19

Kensi

Officer Daniels felt bad for us, so he gave Aftermath and me some extra blankets and pillows during the night. These were a lot softer and didn't scratch my skin. Gratefully, I made a mental note to talk to Capone about doing something for Officer Daniels. If things go the way they do, I can imagine shit is going to hit the fan with this department and who knows how far up the ladder the corruption goes.

I awaken from the commotion on the other side of the door. Shaking Aftermath, I whisper, "Aftermath, wake up. Something is happening."

Aftermath groans before rolling over, "Fuck, this floor sucks ass." He blinks a few times and shakes his head, waking up.

Officer Daniels rises from his chair and walks over to our cell. He stands in front of the doors with his arms crossed over his muscular chest as if he's protecting us from whatever is going on out there.

The metal door they dragged Aftermath through last night opens and Capone strolls in with Blayze, Torch and my father. I scramble to my feet, not knowing what is happening.

Capone nods his head to Officer Daniels, "Release them."

"I don't have the authority." Daniels stands tall, not wavering.

"I do. Now release these two or I'll have your badge too," Capone threatens.

"I'd do what he says," I whisper to Daniels.

Capone, Torch, Blayze and my dad glance at me. My dad looks tired and ready to throw in the flag. "Lil' Kay, are you OK?"

"I'm fine, Dad. Officer Daniels did his best to keep us comfortable." I answer.

Capone nods his head once before looking back to Daniels. "Are you going to let them out or am I going to have to do it for you?" The menace in his voice is unmistakable.

Officer Daniels peers around the four men before speaking. He keeps his voice low, "Where's the Sheriff?" The fear in his voice is unmistakable.

"Sheriff Long is currently being occupied by the FBI. He's been taken in for questioning about missing women and girls recently," my dad answers.

The stress on Officer Daniels' shoulders lifts and he nods his head, "It's about fucking time." He pulls his keys out of the pocket of his pants and unlocks our cell without saying another word.

Riding Through Life   J. Lynn Lombard

Aftermath steps out before me, holding my hand and pulling me with him. "Thank you, Prez. How did you manage this?"

"Let's just say the wrong Sheriff arrested two of my own." I open my mouth to question Capone but my dad's gaze catches my attention and he shakes his head.

Snapping my mouth shut, I turn to Officer Daniels. "Thank you for not being a giant prick last night. It's appreciated the way you handled yourself and treated us and we won't forget it."

"I wish it never came to this with the two of you and I wish you the best of luck," Daniels responds. There is something he isn't saying and I really want to interrogate him about it but one look from Capone has me keeping my mouth shut. His black eyes bore into me, telling me to stay quiet. So, with all the power I can muster, I keep my mouth shut.

Aftermath leads me out of the holding cells, and we walk through the metal door into a long corridor. The slapping of our shoes and boots is the only noise echoing through the hallway. We reach another door and Capone pulls it open. We enter the front lobby of the precinct and there is so much chaos surrounding us that my ears hurt. FBI Agents are scattered through the entire area, pulling boxes and boxes of files. Officers are handcuffed to the benches and stripped of their weapons.

I spot Lynn handcuffed next to an officer and I can't help laughing my ass off. Her left cheek and right eye are black and blue, and her make-up is smearing down her face like she's been crying. When she spots Aftermath and me, she starts rattling the handcuffs, trying to get out, making a spectacle of herself. Three FBI Agents restrain her again and a twisted part of me wishes they'd tase her skanky ass.

So many questions whirl around in my brain, and I do everything I can to keep them to myself, but once we're out of here and I'm married to Aftermath, I will demand these questions to be answered.

The desk Sergeant looks baffled and directs the FBI where to put things or to find them.

Everyone stops what they're doing when the door slams shut behind us. It's so quiet you can hear a pin drop. One man I recognize as the guy who hit me and kidnapped me and my dad walks up to us and holds his hand out, offering to shake my dad's hand.

"What in the fuck are you doing?" I hiss and knock his offered hand away. "After what you did, do you think we'd shake your hand?"

"Ms. Donovan, I understand your hostility," the asshole starts but I interrupt him.

"My hostility?" I step forward and he steps back until his back is against the wall. "My hostility?" I poke my finger in his chest. "You kidnapped my dad and me and gave me a concussion and you think you understand *my hostility?!*"

"Tiger." One word from Aftermath pulls me back from the rage clouding my vision.

Riding Through Life   J. Lynn Lombard

"Aftermath, this is the man who knocked me out, gave me a concussion and kidnapped me and my dad. So don't *Tiger* me." I'm pissed and want my revenge on the man who caused me pain.

Aftermath steps forward and rests his big hands on my shoulders. He squeezes gently, trying to calm me down. Leaning forward, Aftermath's lips brush my ear while his heat hits my back. "I understand your frustration, but you need to let us handle this. He will get what he deserves for putting his hands on you, but punching an FBI Agent in a police station will only get you arrested again and we have a wedding to get to. Now, put those loveable claws away and come with me."

"Do you promise?" I ask, turning my head so I can stare into Aftermath's eyes.

"I promise, Tiger. He will not get away with putting his hands on my woman." The glare he sends to the agent makes me smile. Leave it to Aftermath to rein me back in.

"Now that that's settled let's get the fuck out of here before we all get arrested." Torch chuckles. "If I don't come home, my Ol' Lady will burn this shithole to the ground."

"With you in it," Blayze quips.

"You got that right," Torch confirms.

The six of us leave the precinct without incident and head to the Clubhouse. I'm on the back of

Riding Through Life   J. Lynn Lombard

Aftermath's bike holding onto him tight. Capone and Blayze are in front of us and Torch is next to us. My dad is driving his pick-up behind us. Once we clear the county line limits, Trigger, Derange, Bones and Tiny meet us.

We get to the Clubhouse with little time to spare. I hop off Aftermath's bike and Nadia with Matthew, Danyella, Monica, Daisy and Jezebelle drag me into the Clubhouse, walking a million miles an hour. I'm exhausted and desperately need a shower, but I get that time is moving fast so I let them drag me away.

"We have three hours to get you ready for your wedding," Nadia explains as I open Aftermath's and my room. "So, there will be no fraternizing with Aftermath. That goes for all of you ladies too. Exleigh and Syvannah have the older kids and they're getting MJ and Jaxson ready. Nina will be taking Matthew from me in a little while to get him ready so Red and I can get ready too."

"First thing you need to do is shower," Daisy says plugging her nose. "You smell like Tequila and jail."

I giggle and shrug my shoulders. "Can't help it, trouble always finds me."

"Well, skip the trouble today and focus on marrying that hunk out there," Jezebelle replies. She swats my butt and shoves me toward the bathroom. "And don't take too long."

"Yes, Mom." I salute Jezebelle like an asshole. I shut and lock the door before anyone can come in and interrupt me.

Riding Through Life   J. Lynn Lombard

    I take a quick shower, shaving all the important parts and do a quick rinse of my hair, trying to get the jailhouse odor off. Once I'm clean and hair-free, I turn the water off and step out of the shower. Drying off, I open the bathroom door and for the next few hours, I'm poked, prodded, pinched, squeezed and ready to say *I do*.

Riding Through Life   J. Lynn Lombard

Riding Through Life   J. Lynn Lombard

Chapter 20

Aftermath

Capone called Church as soon as my kickstand was down and Kensi was whisked away by the Ol' ladies. They'll be busy for a while so we have time before we need to be at the beach.

Everyone is in attendance today, including the prospects and the table is full for this meeting. Knight and Seth are standing against the wall with Torch's twin brother, Jax. Last I knew, Jax hadn't decided if he wanted to become a member or not, but with him here, it means he's made his decision and Torch will be sponsoring him. Kensi's dad is here too, which has my attention. Why is a non-member in Church?

"How did you get us out?" I ask, instead of asking the real question why Donovan is here. Yeah, he's going to be my father-in-law in a few hours but he's still on the legal side of the law.

"Well, that's the thing." Capone lights up a cigarette and exhales before continuing. "I didn't get you out. Donovan did." He points to Donovan leaning against the wall. He's wearing faded blue jeans and a hoodie.

Riding Through Life   J. Lynn Lombard

Completely different than his normal attire of business suits and dress pants.

"What? How?" I lean forward and rest my hands on the scarred table. "Please don't tell me he went back to work for those suits."

Capone taps his cigarette ash in the ashtray, "No, he didn't, but he did agree to help them bring down this ring. I'll let him explain more."

Donovan moves forward so he is addressing the whole room. He looks tired with dark circles under his eyes and his neatly styled salt and pepper hair is sticking up all over the place. "When I called Capone to help find that missing girl, I got a tip from someone working at the Sherrif's office in Orange County on where she might have been. I followed the tip to discover Sherrif Long and several of his deputies were involved with the Mexican Cartel. When they failed to deliver security to the Cartel, the Cartel demanded several women of certain types. They had to be young, smart and naive. Once the quota for women was filled by Long and his cronies, they thought they'd be free of the Cartel. Well, as you all know, that's not how it works. So, Long got a brilliant idea to try and pin this Cartel shit on you guys and planted Lynn in Nadia's dance studio.

"Only Long didn't realize the obsession Lynn has had with the Royal Bastards. She particularly had her sights set on Aftermath, not realizing I was Kensi's dad. We don't know why she targeted you and Kensi but here we are. She's in custody with an ass-kicking by my daughter."

"What does this have to do with the FBI though?" I ask. I don't want him going down that rabbit hole, not only for Kensi's sake but the asshole is growing on me and I don't want anything bad happening to him.

"At first, the FBI thought I was the local sheriff abducting these women, which is why they broke into my house and took Kensi and me. When we escaped and came here, I helped Red and Bones uncover who really was behind it and agreed to work with them to bring Long down. But I also told them I want my pound of flesh in Mitchell for hurting my daughter."

"The director wasn't too keen on letting an ex-agent and current agent battle it out, but she's cool like that and will allow me to have my time in the ring with that prick. They owe me this and more for how they treated me since Kensi was missing years ago. That's it. I'm done with the FBI and want to help rescue women like you all do. That's my purpose in life. To be here for my daughter and our little family and help you guys do what you do." Donovan leans back against the wall and releases a deep breath.

I'm shocked by all this information but pleased that Kensi will still have her dad in her life. That he won't sell us out to further his career. That in itself tells me what kind of man Donovan is.

"Do I still have to call you Sheriff or can I call you Pops?" I ask standing up and facing Donovan. I'm being a smartass but it's also a serious question. I've never had a father figure in my life before.

Riding Through Life   J. Lynn Lombard

Donovan steps to me with his arms crossed over his chest. "You make my daughter happy, Aftermath. But if you fuck up like you did, Pops or not, I will blister your ass." He pulls me in for a long hug and I fight back all the emotions flooding to the surface.

"Thanks, Pops." I hug him back and take my seat.

"Now that the biggest issue is out of the way, we have a new member to prospect and a wedding to get to. Everyone, say hey to Jax. He is officially a Prospect for the Royal Bastards MC." Torch flings a cut at Jax who catches it and immediately puts it on.

"Thanks," Jax responds, running his hands over the leather.

"Does this mean Rose will become an Ol' Lady?" Trigger asks, wiggling his eyebrows.

"If and when Jax patches over, yes, Rose will become his Ol' Lady. Shit, Trigger, they're fucking married." Torch slaps his palms on the table.

"Just making sure things won't be weird around here." Trigger shrugs.

"No weirdness. They've been here plenty of times over the last few years and there is zero desire between Rose and me, you fuckhead." Torch slaps Trigger on the back of the head and everyone laughs.

Capone slams his gavel onto the table, shutting everyone up. "Now that that fucked up shit is out of the way, let's get Aftermath to the beach to marry his Tiger. We're all riding our bikes out there together. Knight,

Riding Through Life   J. Lynn Lombard
Seth and Jax will be bringing all the ladies and kids in the SUVs. We'll get you hitched, go to the Royal Casino to celebrate and send you two off on your honeymoon." Capone slams the gavel three times on the table and we all file out of Church together.

We arrive at the beach an hour later. The SUVs are already here with the Ol' Ladies and the kids. I don't see Kensi or Nadia, but they're probably in the tent to the left of the area.

The sun is just setting over the horizon, creating a purple and pink backdrop. Luckily the weather has held out and there is only a small crisp in the air for New Year's Eve. Not too cold and not too hot.

The Ol' Ladies were here earlier and set up chairs and an altar for Kensi and me to be married under. Two dozen chairs, twelve on each side, face the Pacific Ocean lined with white lace and purple satin. Kensi didn't want a big wedding, just our close family.

In the front row on the right is my mom and she is wearing an elegant silver gown that sparkles when she walks with her hair done up in a stylish twist and gold hoop earrings. Pearl, Trigger, Tiny with his kitten Peanut, and Syvannah are sitting behind my mom. Derange, Jezebelle and Seth are behind them.

To the left Zack, Kensi's dad, will sit once he brings her down the aisle. He is wearing a pair of black dress slacks and a silver dress shirt that matches my mom's dress. Kensi didn't want to invite her mom and little brother, which I understood. Sitting behind Zack

Riding Through Life   J. Lynn Lombard

are Capone and Danyella with Nina. Then Blayze and Monica are on the other side of Nina. Torch and Daisy are near the back with Knight, Jax and Rose.

Pretty Boy, Bones, Knight and Exleigh are standing up in the back, keeping an eye on our surroundings and the kids in the wedding occupied. Dagger is in his spot at the front of the altar, preparing to marry us.

Music begins playing and Red walks down the aisle, taking his place to the right of the altar. Mara Jean and Naomi walk down the aisle wearing purple dresses and dropping flowers as they go. Next comes Jaxson bringing the rings wearing a little Royal Bastards cut, a white shirt and dark jeans.

Nadia comes after Jaxson, wearing a long strapless purple gown that fits her like a second skin. From the flame in Red's cheeks and the heated look in both their eyes, we might be welcoming another baby soon.

Once Nadia takes her place to the right of the altar then I take my place at the front and stay turned, facing the ocean. Red is standing next to me, both of us are in our cuts, a clean white t-shirt underneath and black tight-fitting jeans with our boots.

The music changes to *Just Pretend* by *Bad Omens* and I listen as bodies rise. Once the tempo kicks in, I turn to find Kensi standing at the end of the aisle. Her white satin gown clings to every curve of her beautiful body. The sides of her dark hair are pinned out of her face and her mesmerizing blue and green eyes are sparkling with mischief and love.

Riding Through Life   J. Lynn Lombard

The sight before me takes my breath away. Kensi walks down the aisle toward me with her head held high. One hand is looped through her dad's and the other is clutching her bouquet.

She moves toward me with grace and elegance. As I watch her make her way to me, it hits me hard. Everything I love about her is all wrapped up in a tiny, yet mouthy package that isn't afraid to speak her mind and love with all her heart. My eyes tear up and my heart is hammering inside my chest at my beautiful bride-to-be.

Kensi and Zack reach us and I step forward. He releases her hand with fresh tears in his eyes. "You take care of my Lil' Kay or I will hunt you down and castrate you." People near the front row hear Zack's threat and they let out a low chuckle.

"I will love her more than my own life," I vow. Zack kisses Kensi on the side of the head and places her hand in mine. Then he takes his seat in the front row.

We turn to face Dagger and Kensi lets out a squeak of awe. The setting sun is casting beautiful shades of deep purples and pinks. As Dagger gives us our blessing and honors us as husband and wife, a lonely ray of sunlight breaks through the clouds and shines onto our family before disappearing. A blessing in disguise.

Riding Through Life   J. Lynn Lombard

Riding Through Life   J. Lynn Lombard

Epilogue

Kensi 1 year later

Our house is finally finished and Aftermath and I moved in a couple of days ago. We are hosting a get together with all of the Royal Bastards MC in attendance. Aftermath bought the property to the left of Red and Nadia's house, which was finished two months ago, just in time for Nadia to spring a little surprise on all of us by needing another bedroom added. Red is freaking out but Nadia is excited to give Matthew a baby brother or sister.

I set the food on the table in the backyard when Aftermath swoops me off my feet. I instinctively wrap my legs around his waist and pepper his face with kisses. Being in his arms never gets tiring or old.

"I have something I want to show you, Tiger." Aftermath growls against my neck. My panties dampen from the deep timber of Aftermath's voice vibrating against my skin.

"Hmm... Our guests will be here soon." I whine pressing myself down on the hardness behind the zipper

Riding Through Life   J. Lynn Lombard

of his jeans. I want whatever Aftermath wants to show me, twenty-four seven.

"It'll be quick and our guests can wait."

Aftermath carries me into our house, slamming the door with the heel of his boot and sets me on the kitchen counter. He works my tight jeans down my legs until he flings them off along with my panties. The cold marble against my skin makes me gasp.

We've christened every room in this house over the last couple of days and we're about to do it again on the marble countertop. Aftermath kisses me hard. We're a mess of tongue and teeth scraping against each other. I thread my fingers through his hair and gently tug, causing him to groan. Aftermath reaches between us and his hand cups my sex, feeling the heat coming off me. His fingers explore me, causing me to moan and climb to an orgasm.

Before I can comprehend what's happening, Aftermath's belt is unbuckled and he drops his pants. He slides my ass to the edge of the countertop and enters me with one smooth thrust. I lock my heels around his backside, pushing him into me deeper.

He thrusts hard and fast, causing me to claw and scratch his back as my orgasm takes over and I fall over the edge with Aftermath falling right behind me. Once I am breathing normally again, I grasp Aftermath's face and shower him with kisses.

"There's something I need to tell you," I say, not letting him pull out yet.

Riding Through Life   J. Lynn Lombard

"What's that, Tiger?" Aftermath nuzzles my neck.

"In about nine months, we won't be able to do this anywhere we want for eighteen years."

Aftermath stops nuzzling my neck. He pulls his lips away from my neck to stare into my eyes. "Are you serious?"

"One hundred percent serious."

I can feel Aftermath growing hard again inside of me. "I'm going to be a dad?"

"One of the best dads out there," I respond.

Aftermath kisses me hard and begins moving again. His thrusts are long and deep and bring me to the edge quickly. We both shout out in pleasure as we tip over the edge together.

Riding the storm of life, Aftermath and I come out stronger on the other side. Now and always, he will be my ride or die as I am his.

Riding Through Life   J. Lynn Lombard

Riding Through Life   J. Lynn Lombard
       Thank you!

First off, I want to thank my husband for always encouraging me to keep going and asking if I've made millions yet so we can retire lol! Next are my 2 kids. You both are resilient, courageous and honestly the best thing your dad and I could ever do. Don't ever change no matter what.

Thank you to all you beautiful readers! I had so much fun writing this book and bringing Kensi and Aftermath's dream wedding to life. (Even if Kensi keeps getting into trouble!)

I hope you enjoyed reading about my Royal Bastards as much as I enjoy writing them. I know shit's been so hard for all of us, dealing with life and even though I struggled to find my mojo, I really hope you all enjoy these stories and the world we created as an escape.

Please, if you want to thank an Indy author, the best way is either an email, message or even leaving a review on any platform so others can see how much you enjoy it. I know I love hearing from my readers, and I appreciate every single one of you.

You might have seen some familiar names in here and that's because some of the other RBMC authors let me borrow their characters and cameo appearances from some of my other published books as well. Make sure you check out their books (and mine) too!

***

Riding Through Life   J. Lynn Lombard

Thank you to Sarah, Michelle, Joy, Monica, Elise and Krista for keeping my ass straight and being as excited as I am on each book. You all are my Rockstars and I'm so grateful for you to be in my life.

Nikki, Crimson and all the other Royal Bastards authors. Who would have thought a small idea over five years ago would turn into something this big and phenomenal?

Without you inviting me in during that signing in Ann Arbor, Crimson, I would never have had this opportunity to work with all of you and I will forever be grateful for your invite. Every single RBMC author rocks each book and I'm overwhelmed with gratitude to each of you. Ok I'm done with the sappy shit.

Thank you once more for picking up this book and giving me a chance!

Books written by J. Lynn Lombard

Royal Bastards MC

Blayze's Inferno

Amazon: https://amzn.to/2DSLZ1x

Capone's Chaos

Amazon: https://amzn.to/34QUrNS

Capone's Christmas

Amazon: https://amzn.to/34QUrNs

Torch's Torment

Amazon: https://amzn.to/2Vh2Qax

Derange's Destruction

Amazon: https://amzn.to/3uVAi5z

Jaded Red

Amazon: https://bit.ly/30G7Fcn

Global Outlaw Syndicate

Deadly Rose:

Amazon: https://amzn.to/3lvyFCt

Riding Through Life   J. Lynn Lombard
Fallen Spades MC

Kayne's Fury:

Get it here: Amazon: https://amzn.to/2DbXmAl

Blayde's Betrayal

Get it here: Amazon https://amzn.to/2Z0yGoc

Stryker's Salvation

Get it here: Amazon https://amzn.to/2lnXZKV

Rooster's Redemption

Get it here: Amazon https://bit.ly/4de7Syg

Ace's Ascension

Get it here: https://bit.ly/3LReJuB

All are #FreeonKU

Find the stories that started all of this in the completed

Racing Dirty Series

Thrust (book 1) Amazon: https://amzn.to/2AwrgJ7

Torque (book 2) Amazon: https://amzn.to/2H0JugS

Turbulence (book 3) Amazon: https://amzn.to/2KNuTaj

Riding Through Life J. Lynn Lombard
Collection of Badass short stores

Keep it Real: https://a.co/d/gT0xDHv

Made in the USA
Columbia, SC
18 February 2025